The Consequences of Careless Cyber Crime

Ray Filby

==

The Consequences of Careless Cyber Crime

Publisher : Midhurst

Published by Midhurst

Midhurst.
2, Freers Mews,
Warwick,
Warwickshire,
CV34 6DP

ISBN 978-1-9168947-2-3

http://midhurstpublishing.uk

Acknowledgements

The author would like to acknowledge the help and advice he has received in writing this book from several friends, some of whom had first-hand experience of technologies and institutions which impact on the unfolding narrative contained in this story.

First and foremost, he would like to thank his wife, Sue, for proof-reading the manuscript. Thanks are due for the suggestions made by Richard Lyttle, Val Brant and Martyn Colliver whose professional advice was gratefully received. Special thanks are due too, to the author's writers' group, Mari Cunliffe, Dalbir Khaira, Wendy Philips and Karen Wightman, who encouraged him in the process of writing this with their valuable suggestions. Indeed, it was Mari who encouraged him to write this book in the first place as a sequel to 'A Church like Cluedo' so that the developing career of police officer, Christine Powers could be followed.

Contents

Chapter 1

<u>'C & E Software Enterprises'</u>

"We have a problem. How are we going to sort this one?"

"We're problem solvers. We'll find a way of dealing with it."

An animated discussion was taking place between two energetic young men who projected a certain arrogance which seemed to convey the impression that *'we're alpha males and don't we know it'*. The discussion was taking place in their workplace which was evidently a hi-tech environment. There were about half a dozen workstations with at least three displaying activated computer screens, one of which appeared to be scrolling through pages of data while a printer in another corner was churning out printouts of carefully formatted information. A Cona coffee flask bubbled away on a bench under the window. The flask was surrounded by a number of mugs, some of which needed to be washed, a jug of milk and a tin of biscuits. The office was well lit with natural light shining through frosted glass windows. On the other side of a half open door issuing into a smaller office, a young woman was seated at a computer keyboard.

The taller of the two young men, Henry Erikson, wore jeans and a pale green tee shirt across which was emblazoned :-

$$\sqrt{-1} \qquad 2^3 \qquad \Sigma \qquad \pi$$

Those of a mathematical persuasion will know that this can be interpreted as :-

I   ate   some   pie

Henry was tall, well-built and had thick blond hair. He wore rimless glasses. Henry had graduated three years earlier from Imperial College with a computer science degree and, with his business partner, Courtney Cavendish, had founded 'C & E Software Enterprises' which offered programming advice, designed websites and carried out computer repairs.

Henry's partner, Courtney Cavendish, was nearly the same height as Henry but of slimmer build. He wore grey flannels and a cream coloured polo-neck jumper. Henry wore suede loafers while Courtney preferred well-polished black boots for his footwear. Courtney's dark hair was neatly combed and brushed across, creating a left side parting.

"Well, we haven't got much time," Henry continued. "The ultimatum we were served gives us until tomorrow to work out a plan of action."

Courtney moved across to the side office and closed the door. Evidently, they didn't want their admin assistant to eavesdrop their conversation as they continued to talk in quieter tones.

Their admin assistant, Olivia Clark, was a pretty twenty something who had joined the firm nine months earlier after completing a business studies course at the local technical college. She was tastefully dressed in an exquisitely designed sweater and a navy skirt. Her rich chestnut brown hair cascaded to her shoulders in a myriad of tight curls. In the interests of comfort, Olivia had kicked off the patent leather, ridiculously high heeled shoes which were fashionable among young women of her age and they rested on the ground under her desk. Her office was plain but Olivia had added a few feminine touches, - two landscape pictures of the Cotswold countryside hung on the wall opposite her desk and a vase of freshly cut flowers stood on the windowsill.

The fourth member of the team, Hamish McIntosh, was not in the office that morning. Hamish had only been with the firm for six months but Henry and Courtney felt that they had been successful in recruiting him. Henry had a degree in maths and computing from Birmingham University and was clearly a very bright young man. Today, he was out visiting a client who needed advice on the website he had commissioned the firm to design for him. Hamish was proud of his Scottish ancestry and displayed this by wearing bright tartan jackets, the tartans representing the various clans from whom Hamish claimed to be descended.

The following day, the office was unlocked just before 8:30 am by Olivia who was always the first arrival. Hamish usually arrived at the office ten minutes after Olivia but he hadn't arrived by 8:45 am. This was unusual as Hamish was seldom late. Olivia checked the diary to see whether Hamish had an appointment that day. Yes, it appeared that he was due to be out mid-morning but the nature of his errand wasn't clear. As usual, Henry and Courtney arrived within five minutes of each other at about 9:00 am. Courtney looked round the office.

"What, no Hamish?"

The question was addressed to Olivia who replied in the negative.

At 9:30, Henry and Courtney appeared to be somewhat agitated.

"Olivia, please could you ring Hamish's home to see why he hasn't shown up this morning," asked Henry.

Hamish lived at home with his parents.

Olivia made the call and reported that Hamish had left for work as usual that morning.

"OK then, please could you try Hamish's mobile to find out where he might be."

Olivia tried this number but had to report that Hamish's mobile seemed to be dead.

"Well, if he doesn't show up in the next ten minutes, Courtney and I will have to keep his appointment. We can't let down a valued client."

Quarter of an hour later, Henry and Courtney had donned their jackets and made for the door. Courtney was carrying a slim laptop computer.

"We're sorry to be leaving you to look after the office alone," apologised Henry. "We know that lone working should be avoided except in the case of an emergency but Hamish's absence has left us with no choice. Will you be OK? If any calls come in which you can't deal with, tell them that we'll be back by mid-afternoon if not earlier. If anything comes up which seems particularly urgent, call us on our mobiles."

Olivia assured them that lone working wasn't a problem for her. Thus reassured, Henry and Courtney left the office.

Only two calls came in that morning, one from someone asking if he could bring in his laptop to be checked over as it wasn't behaving as it should, and the other from Hamish's parents asking if he had shown up. Olivia had to tell them that there'd been no sign of Hamish.

Chapter 2

<u>Oakenhampton Police Station</u>

The police station stood in the middle of a row of up-market shops in the town of Oakenhampton. Oakenhampton was a small Cotswold town. The police station stood out as one of the few building in the High Street which wasn't a shop. 'Police Station' engraved on the lintel above the entrance wasn't the only indication of the building's function. The streetlight outside the building was blue.

Detective Inspector Christine Powers was an able and shrewd detective working at this station. She had been given an exceptional dispensation to work on an enquiry into her sister, Joan's, murder and had gained considerable kudos for her part in the identification and arrest of the murderer. (*Joan had been a police officer at Oakenhampton police station some ten years earlier.*) Christine's promotion had soon followed. The senior officer at the police station was Chief Inspector Colin Whittaker who had earlier been Christine's partner when she was a Detective Constable.

Chief Inspector Whittaker invited Christine into his office.

"We've had a call about a missing person," explained Colin. "They phoned yesterday to say that their son hadn't shown up at work or returned home in the evening. He'd left for work in a perfectly normal way that morning. I told them that a person couldn't be classified as missing until they hadn't been seen for at least twenty-four hours. Well, they phoned again this morning to say the twenty-four hours were up and could I do something. I'd be grateful if you could pay them a visit, Christine, and see if there's anything we could do at this early stage. The couple are a Mr and Mrs McIntosh and they live in Cowslip Crescent."

The Chief Inspector handed Joan the missing person log which included these details. Christine made her way to no 7, Cowslip Crescent, where the door was opened by a very worried looking woman. Joan showed her her warrant card and introduced herself as Detective Inspector Powers. She was ushered into a tidy sitting room where a similarly worried looking gentleman was seated on an armchair. He stood and motioned Christine to another armchair while Mrs. McIntosh took her seat on the sofa.

"I understand that your son, Hamish, left for work yesterday," started Christine, "and hasn't been seen since."

"That's right," said Mrs. McIntosh. She spoke with the suspicion of a Scottish brogue. "The secretary from his workplace phoned sometime after nine o'clock to say he hadn't turned up and to ask if Hamish was all right."

"Have you any reason to think that anything was wrong?"

Mr. McIntosh replied, "Nothing specific that we can explain but last week he did seem a bit disillusioned about his work."

Mrs. McIntosh came back into the conversation.

"Normally, he was very happy at his job. He's been with the firm for about six months and often came home, glowing about what he had achieved that day but, as Andy said, we did feel that something was wrong last week. He's good with computers which is what he works on. We were so proud to attend his graduation from University last year and were delighted when he landed this job which seemed to be just ideal for him."

"Has Hamish ever gone missing before or is there anything else which might have been worrying him?" asked Christine.

"No, nothing like this has ever happened before. He hasn't got a particular girlfriend so we don't think there can be any problem in that direction. We're at a loss to know what could possibly have happened." she replied.

"If someone goes missing and is determined not to be found, they can be very difficult to track down but we'll do our best to find Hamish. We'll make a general enquiry round the hospitals but if he's had an accident, the hospital would have been bound to inform you. Meanwhile, I'll call in at his place of work to see if they can throw any light on the mystery. Where did he work?" asked Christine as she concluded this conversation.

"C & E Software Enterprises," said Mrs McIntosh. "It's in the high street not far from the Police Station."

"I know the complex where this business occupies a suite. I'll make my way over there now" said Christine. Before she bid her farewell to an obviously greatly concerned couple, Christine took down the details and registration number of the car Hamish was driving when he left home the previous day. It was a red Fiat 500.

Christine arrived at the smart block which evidently accommodated a number of firms in the high technology sphere. She pressed the bell-push against 'C & E Software Enterprises' and a female voice came down the inter-com restating the name of the business.

"I'm Detective Inspector Powers," answered Christine. "I've come in connection with an enquiry we are making into the disappearance of one of your employees."

"Please come up. We're on the second floor."

Christine pushed the door as the buzzer sounded and ascended the stairs. The clear label showed her which door to enter and she found Henry and Courtney waiting of her. Christine showed her warrant card as she introduced herself and explained her business.

"I've just come from the home of Mr and Mrs McIntosh who are concerned over the whereabouts of their son, Hamish, who's gone missing. I gather he worked here and I wonder whether you could throw any light on this mystery."

Henry answered, "We're as baffled as Hamish's parents about his disappearance. He's always been so reliable and conscientious. He's an excellent worker. He just didn't show up yesterday. That's not like Hamish at all."

Christine asked the expected questions about any apparent worries Hamish might have had, any strangeness of behaviour, but neither Henry nor Courtney could come up with anything unusual which could explain Hamish's absence.

"Does anyone else work here who might have some relevant information?" asked Christine.

Courtney went to the side office door and asked Olivia to join them. The only thing Olivia came up with was that she felt Hamish seemed to be out of sorts the previous few days. Christine noticed Henry slightly flinch as Olivia came out with this and she formed the impression that Henry and Courtney were hiding something. Anyway, Christine thanked them for their time and bid farewell as she returned to the Police Station to report back to Chief Inspector Whittaker.

Chapter 3

<u>Investigation into Hamish's Disappearance</u>

On Monday morning, Chief Inspector Colin Whittaker set up a meeting between himself, Detective Inspector Christine Powers and Detective Sergeant Bill Matthews to discuss the missing person's case on their books. Bill was a young police officer who exuded enthusiasm. He had graduated in economics from Manchester University. Bill was of average height and build but seemed possessed with boundless energy. His hair was auburn and his face bore just the suspicion of freckles. As a uniformed officer, Bill had impressed with his immaculate appearance, his attention to detail and his intuitive assessment of what lay behind complex situations. Bill's qualities marked him out as a potentially brilliant detective and he was transferred from uniform to plainclothes work where he quickly rose to the rank of detective sergeant. Bill was Christine's normal partner but he'd been on leave the previous week when Hamish's disappearance had been reported and hadn't therefore been present when Christine had visited C & E Software Enterprises or Hamish's parents. Chief Inspector Colin Whittaker outlined the very limited information available to bring Bill up to speed.

"So where do we go from here?" asked Colin to evoke some suggestions from the two detectives.

"We could have a look through the traffic surveillance camera footage on the day Hamish was reported missing," suggested Christine. "We might get a sighting of Hamish's car."

"What sort of car would that be?" enquired Bill.

"A red Fiat 500, registration KG 12 LPR."

"A fairly old model then," commented Bill.

That's to be expected," explained Christine. "Hamish had only been out of college for less than a year."

There were two surveillance cameras covering Oakenhampton High Street, located near the traffic lights at each end of town. Sure enough, Hamish's car showed up on each of these cameras, one showing it coming into town and the other leaving. Apart from seeing that the driver was wearing a reddish coloured jacket, there wasn't much else to identify the driver.

"Well," said Colin, "It looks as if Hamish drove straight through town on the day of his disappearance."

"Not necessarily," said Bill. "Let's look at the time stamps on the surveillance cameras to get a more detailed picture of his transit."

Christine nodded. She was glad to see that Bill was back and on the ball. Yes, it was obvious that knowing the times that Hamish entered and left town was crucial. The time stamps showed that Hamish had passed the camera as he entered town at 8:35 am and didn't pass the camera on the other side of town until 9:40 am.

"It takes less than five minutes to drive through town on a normal day," commented Christine. "This means that there's almost an hour's unaccounted for time when Hamish must have been still in town before his car was picked up as leaving, but, from the statements of those I met at his office, he doesn't appear to have shown up there."

"We'll put out a wanted car alert in the hope that a patrol car might encounter Hamish's car," said the Chief Inspector. "Current technology means that the registration numbers of cars of interest to the police are stored on patrol cars' on-board computers. Otherwise, we've not much to go on. Let's hope that Hamish realises the anguish he's causing his parents and gets in touch soon".

Two days later, Hamish's car was discovered. Mr Grimond, the landlord of the White Hart, a pub located on the Stow Road and not too far from Oakenhampton, reported that a car had been abandoned in the pub's car park. While it would appear that cars were often left overnight in the car park, they were usually gone within 24 hours. Mr Grimond was particularly worried about this car as there appeared to be blood stains on the front two seats.

Christine and Bill made their way to the White Hart where they were greeted by Mr. Grimond who seemed a very jovial good-natured sort of pub landlord. Yes, the red Fiat must have arrived at the car park at about 10 a.m. the previous Tuesday. The driver of the car had come in and had a coffee. He appeared to be quite a chatty sort of person, wanting to engage in conversation with Mr Grimond. Mr Grimond was sure that he was the driver of the red Fiat because there was hardly anybody else in the pub at that time and the other two cars in the car park were well known to Mr Grimond. In spite of the fact that they had chatted for a while, the only distinguishing feature that Mr Grimond could recall about the driver was that he was wearing a red tartan jacket. He thought that the tartan was Royal Stuart but he wasn't an expert on clan tartans. Mr Grimond would have left the car there a bit longer before reporting it. The cars in the White Hart car park weren't usually abandoned but just left there and collected by their owners within days. However, when he went to investigate this car, he had the suspicion that the stains on the front seats were blood stains and that's why he contacted the police.

Mr. Grimond accompanied Christine and Bill as they went to examine the car. Without attempting to open the door, they could see what Mr. Grimond believed to be blood stains. Christine and Bill cordoned off the car with incident tape and Christine contacted forensics to come and examine the car and have it stored in a police compound. They explained to Mr Grimond what they had done and why they were interested in this car. They then thanked him for his information and returned to Oakenhampton.

Two days later, a piece of grim news was received. A dog, who had been being walked by his owner along the Stow Road, had begun to unearth what the dog's owner realised was a plastic body bag. It was buried in a shallow grave by a layby just off the road. The layby must have been part of the main road at some earlier time. It had been replaced by a new road which ran the other side of trees which were now on a traffic island bounded by the new road on one side and what had been the old road on the other. This part of the old road had now become a fairly lengthy layby. Thus, at a quiet time of day, it would have been possible to dig a shallow grave, unobserved by cars passing on the main road. The corpse in the body bag was taken to the mortuary. He was wearing a tartan jacket and had been shot through the temple.

The following day, Christine and Bill had the harrowing task of having to break the news to Mr and Mrs McIntosh. They were ushered into the living room and Christine asked them to sit down. They sat next to each other on the sofa, already braced for receiving bad news. Christine broke the news as gently as she could, stating that a body had been discovered which they felt was likely to be Hamish but formal identification would be needed. Mrs. McIntosh burst into tears. Mr McIntosh put a comforting arm round his wife.

Once Mrs McIntosh had managed to compose herself, Bill explained how Hamish's body had been discovered and that he had clearly been murdered. The McIntoshes had no idea who could possibly have done such a thing. Mr McIntosh was asked to attend the mortuary to formally identify the body. They asked for the names and addresses of all of Hamish's friends who would have to be contacted in case they could throw light on who might have committed this evil deed. Christine enquired as to whether Hamish had a mobile phone or a laptop in the house as information contained on these could help the police in their investigations. Mrs McIntosh went to look in Hamish's room and came back five minutes later. She couldn't find Hamish's phone which she assumed he had on him when he left the house but handed over a slim Dell laptop computer.

After sharing a few more words of consolation and promising to keep the McIntoshes informed of any developments discovered in their search for Hamish's murderer, Christine and Bill made their way to C & E Software Enterprises.

The partners and their admin assistant were naturally shocked by the news. Christine then asked them about timings and where they had been and what they had been doing the day Hamish had gone missing. Bill recorded the information supplied, This indicated that Olivia had arrived first at the office at her usual time of 8:30 am. Hamish had not appeared as expected at 8:45 am and his absence was noted by Henry and Courtney who arrived at about 9:00 am as they usually did. In view of his not having called in to collect the computer to take to the client he had been appointed to see, Henry and Courtney decided they would have to go themselves. They estimated that they had left the office at about 10:00 am and returned mid-afternoon. They had gone to return this laptop computer which had been collected for repair by Hamish from the client a few days earlier. Olivia had not left the office but had received a few phone calls during the morning.

Christine asked for the name and address of this client. He was a Mr Morgan living near Stow-on-the-Wold. For the sake of thoroughness, they paid a visit to Mr Morgan. Mr Morgan took some time to answer the door. He was supported by crutches and clearly had mobility problems. Yes, Henry and Courtney had called in with his computer which had been collected a few days earlier by someone Mr Morgan described as a younger, fresh faced member of the firm. Their visit was unexpected but Mr Morgan was pleased to have his computer returned within a week rather than the fortnight wait which he'd been told was the time needed to effect the repair. The computer had had to be collected for repair because Mr Morgan couldn't drive and had difficulties in using public transport. The taller of the two men who called with the computer had loaded antivirus software on to the computer while the other checked for his WiFi connection and arranged for the computer to be connected wirelessly to his printer.

Christine and Bill returned to their car to assess the implications of their investigation to date.

"On the face of it," started Christine, "it might initially appear to anyone investigating this murder that Hamish drove from Oakenhampton, straight down the Stow Road to the White Hart. Here he stopped for a coffee and engaged the landlord in chatter. Then he went out to be murdered by person or persons unknown. They took his body to a layby about a mile away and buried his body in a shallow grave by a point in a layby not easily visible from the main road. This sequence of events doesn't really make sense does it?"

"No," agreed Bill. "It could be that the person in the White Hart was not Hamish but the murderer, dressed in Hamish's coat to create the false impression that Hamish himself had stopped at the pub."

"Yes," said Christine. "The person in the pub, possibly working with an accomplice, arrived at the White Hart in their own transport or possibly in Hamish's car, having already murdered Hamish during the time between Hamish entering and leaving Oakenhampton which we can't account for. If they came in their own transport, it wasn't observed in the White Hart carpark by the landlord."

"This suggests that the staff at C & E Software Enterprises are likely suspects" conjectured Bill, "but they have an alibi."

"Yes, but a pretty weak alibi at that," observed Christine. "The errand which Hamish was expected to have carried out that morning, doesn't sound like a prearranged appointment. Courtney and Henry arrived unexpectedly at Mr Morgan's house. It hardly needed two senior people like Henry and Courtney to go to Mr Morgan's to carry out fairly standard setting up procedure for a computer, especially if this required that a young person like Olivia should be left working alone in their office. Of course, they have no alibi for the time elapsing between Hamish's car being seen to enter Oakenhampton High Street and leaving Oakenhampton about an hour later."

"I think our minds are set in the right direction," said Bill "but at present this is all speculation. We've nothing like enough evidence to build up a case and we don't have a motive. How are we going to obtain this evidence? How are we going to discover the motive?"

"That's the problem we now face," responded Christine. "We need to keep our eyes and ears open and our minds alert if we're going to get any further with this case!"

On returning to Oakenhampton, Christine had a look through the files on Hamish's laptop. Nothing there made much sense to Christine except for a file which seemed to contain a large list of clients with details about their addresses, bank accounts, phone numbers and their computer identities. Christine printed out this list and arranged to pass the laptop on to the specialist forensic branch which dealt with computers.

A couple of days later, Chief Inspector Whittaker called Christine and Bill into his office with news he had received from forensics. They had examined the body and the car, and yes, the stains were indeed blood stains which matched the victim's. The steering wheel had been wiped clean but there were plenty of other fingerprints on the door handles, hand brake and gear lever which didn't match the fingerprints they had taken from Hamish's corpse. The layby where the body had been found was quite muddy and the mud matched mud on the wheels of Hamish's car.

Christine then explained to the Chief Inspector that this information fitted in with the theory that she and Bill had developed about the murder. They believed that Hamish may have been threatening to disclose information about Henry and Courtney which would have been very damaging to them. To silence Hamish, they arranged to arrive early in the section of the car park, reserved for C & E Software Enterprises which was secluded and not overlooked, and waited until Hamish arrived. It is possible that they would then have shot Hamish with a gun fitted with a silencer and left him in his car. Henry and Courtney would have gone up to the office just after 9:00 am, their usual time of arrival, and pretended to be surprised that Hamish hadn't arrived for work. They told Olivia that they needed to complete the job Hamish was supposed to be carrying out and they claimed to have left the office at 10:00 am. They went to the car park where one of them could have put on Hamish's jacket and have driven Hamish's car to the White Hart while the other partner followed in his own car. On reaching the White Hart, the partner wearing Hamish's jacket went in to have a coffee. If asked later, the landlord would state that he had served someone wearing a tartan jacket but it would be unlikely for the landlord to have registered any other significant details about the customer. This would have created the impression that Hamish himself had been the customer that morning. The partners would then have driven to the layby and buried Hamish in a body bag they had previously acquired for the purpose before returning to leave Hamish's car in the White Hart car park. They then would have driven to the client whom Hamish was apparently appointed to see and returned his repaired laptop. This provided themselves with a weak alibi. They returned to the office by mid-afternoon.

"This all sounds very plausible," agreed Chief Inspector Whittaker "but at this stage it's just a theory and the motive you suggest is no more than speculation. We need much more evidence before we can make an arrest."

"For a start, we can get the fingerprints of the directors of C & E Software Enterprises," suggested Christine "and we can run another check on the traffic cameras showing the cars leaving Oakenhampton."

"How will we get the fingerprints?" asked Bill. "They're not legally required to supply them."

"No great problem," replied Christine. "I've done this sort of thing before."

That afternoon, Christine and Bill called back at C & E Software Enterprises. They checked on the cars in the firm's reserved parking bays. Olivia obviously walked to work but the two up-market cars were a BMW iX M60 electric vehicle, registration number, ST 21 FGH, and a Jaguar XE, registration number, PR 22 DFR.

They entered the office and were met by Henry and Courtney. Christine explained that they had found something in Hamish's car which they didn't recognise and wondered whether Henry or Courtney could

explain what it was as there was a faint possibility that
this might throw some light on Hamish's murder. She
handed them a cylindrical slide rule.

(This is not something most people will have
encountered, especially as electronic calculators have
made slide rules obsolete. A cylindrical slide rule
consists of a pair of white cylinders which slide in and
out of a central encasing cylinder. Logarithmic scales
are engraved to spiral round the two plastic cylinders.
Because the length of the inscribed scales is so much
greater than the scales on a conventional slide rule, a
cylindrical slide rule will work to an accuracy of three
significant figures which is one more than a straight
slide rule can achieve.)

Christine handed the slide rule to Henry who opened it
out and rotated the cylinders and slid them back and
forth into the casing. He handed the slide rule to
Courtney who similarly manipulated the instrument.
Yes, they both knew what it was although they hadn't
seen one for years and years. They had had no idea that
Hamish possessed such a thing and couldn't see that
this would have any relevance to his murder.

Christine and Bill thanked them for their help and
returned to the station to view the traffic footage of cars
leaving   Oakenhampton   on   the   day   Hamish

disappeared. The BMW they had just seen in the firm's car park was observed to leave Oakenhampton about five minutes after Hamish's red Fiat. It wasn't possible to identify from the footage who was driving each car.

Chapter 4

<u>Other Activities in Oakenhampton</u>

The only means available to Christine and Bill to continue their investigation into Hamish's murder was to contact everyone on the list of the friends which had been provided for them by the McIntoshes. Without exception, Hamish's friends were shocked and saddened by his murder. It appears that he was universally popular and well liked. Christine and Bill had to ask all those they interviewed to state where they were on the Tuesday morning that Hamish had gone missing. They explained that this was a formality they had to comply with in the absence of any definite leads as everyone had to be treated as a suspect until they could be definitely eliminated from the enquiry. For the most part, everyone had been at their place of work and provided sound alibis which could be easily verified. Only one friend, whom Hamish had seen just a couple of days before his death, came up with anything that Christine and Bill considered to be relevant. This friend said that Hamish had confided in him that he was worried that things were going on at his place of work which he considered to be illegal and in which he could become implicated if he didn't take a stand. However, the actual nature of these activities hadn't been disclosed to Hamish's friend. Christine and Bill looked across at each other. This revelation was significant. It reinforced Christine and Bill's theory about a possible motive for the murder.

A further development which they realised would be useful once they were in a position to make an arrest came from Mr Grimond, the landlord of the White Hart. Once he had read in the news about the murder which was associated with the car which had been abandoned in the pub's car park, Mr Grimond had thought back very carefully about the person he had served who had been wearing the tartan jacket. He realised that he had noticed a distinguishing feature which might enable him to make a positive identity of that customer, a small V shaped scar just above the edge of the left eyebrow, a detail which he had overlooked when first interviewed by the police. Christine had left the police station contact details with Mr Grimond at the end of their visit there a few days earlier to enable him to get in touch if he remembered anything he considered to be significant. Mr Grimond was shown a photograph to verify whether or not Hamish was the customer he had served that day. The identification was negative. The photograph definitely did not correspond to Mr Grimond's customer. Again, this was in line with the theory that Christine and Bill had developed about the murder.

A surprising breakthrough in the investigation came as a result of an activity of Christine's which had no obvious direct relevance to the investigation in hand. Christine was a very active member of St Giles, the parish church of Oakenhampton. She was on the Parochial Church Council and involved in many of the church activities. She was popular among all the members of the congregation but her special church friend was Michael Lapworth. Michael had a vetinary practice on the edge of town where he dealt mainly with domestic pets. A larger practice located at the other end of Oakenhampton specialised in farm animals. I wouldn't suggest that Christine and Michael's friendship was of a romantic nature. They were just good friends who enjoyed each other's company. Perhaps the age difference was a factor which limited the depth of their friendship. Christine was thirty and Michael, twenty-six. Even in today's world, some men are foolish enough to think that any woman with whom they are to become romantically involved should be younger than themselves!

When off duty, Christine still observed the world around her with a police officer's eye. When she took her car in to be washed, she noticed that some of those working in the car wash had very limited English and had to refer the customer to the supervisor to deal with the simplest query. Christine was aware that car washes were the sort of business which employed illegal immigrants. Not all illegal immigrants are intercepted by the border patrols and because of their status, these immigrants could become almost slaves of those for whom they worked. Christine enquired of the supervisor how these workers had been recruited. He claimed that they were recruited from the 'Professional, Office and Manual Employment Bureau', an employment agency in Chipping Norton,.

"Do you pay their National Insurance contribution?" Christine asked him.

"Oh no, they're not formally employed here. They're casual labour. At the end of the day, we count out our takings and share the proceeds fairly among ourselves."

Christine wondered just how fair the share-out might have been but didn't pursue the matter. She decided that on the following day, she would pay a visit to the 'Professional, Office and Manual Employment Bureau' in her professional capacity.

At 10 o'clock the following morning, Christine and Bill arrived at the 'Professional, Office and Manual Employment Bureau' and asked to see the manager to whom they introduced themselves and showed their warrant cards. Christine enquired about the workers she had encountered at the car wash, their origin and how much he was paid by the clients who took on these workers. The manager explained that he received £200 for each worker which was the profit their employer believed that they brought to the firm in a fortnight. He knew very little about the origin of these workers apart from what was on their passports. These were passed to him from a larger employment agency organisation working nationally and from whom they'd been recruited, and yes, he still held these passports. The manager was very reluctant to provide details of the larger organisation from whom he recruited workers and told Christine that she had no authority to ask for this information. Christine told the manager that she strongly suspected that he was involved in human trafficking and if she didn't receive the information she requested, he would be investigated by police-officers senior to herself. She explained that they were really interested in the people who were higher up in the human trafficking business and these would be the focus of police investigation rather than someone like himself who was only peripherally involved. With some reluctance, the manager provided her with the limited information he could give her with a request that the police never disclosed from where they had received this information. The manager's contact was known to him only as 'President'. He had no address but just a mobile telephone number.

When they returned to Oakenhampton, Christine and Bill reported to Chief Inspector Colin Whittaker. The information they could give him seemed fairly limited and trivial but Colin seemed very pleased with it.

"Nationally, dealing with people trafficking is a high priority," Colin explained, "and although the information supplied may appear to be very limited, we should be able to do something with the mobile phone numbers. If the contact whose mobile number you've obtained goes by the pseudonym, 'President', he's probably fairly senior in the organisation of human traffickers."

It was not for some months that Christine and Bill realised just how important that information had been. Calls had been intercepted and monitored. The numbers obtained had been shared with Interpol and other European police forces. The objective of the operations that would be planned from information derived from monitoring these calls was not so much to identify the minor players, evil though these may be, but to discover who were the main bosses behind this trade. These bosses remain secluded in the background and were difficult to apprehend because they get others to do their dirty work while remaining concealed. However, once enough information can be derived from phone conversations about the way the people trafficking organisation is working, sufficient evidence may be derived to enable these shadowy but influential background figures to be arrested and a strong case made to get them prosecuted. Thus, some time later, Chris and Bill were delighted to discover that a wave of arrests had been made both in this country and in Europe which included a large number of human trafficking barons.

Chapter 5

<u>The Mini Food Supply Hub</u>

An activity based at St. Giles church and in which both Christine and Michael were heavily involved was the Mini Food Supply Hub. This was set up to provide food for needy families during the Covid epidemic and then the cost of living crisis which followed this. The Mini Food Supply Hub was rather smaller than a conventional Food Bank but had the same objectives in view, to support the many poorer families living in the otherwise affluent Cotswold town of Oakenhampton. The initiator of this project was a Miss Marion Attwood, an energetic lady in her early sixties. When the sharp increase in the cost of living really started to bite and seriously affect the poorer families in the community, Marion declared that it was no good the church preaching a doctrine of love and care if it didn't put resources and effort where its mouth was. Marion was so popular and well liked that she had no difficulty in raising a team of willing helpers, and with their help, Marion set up this Mini Food Supply Hub. She took over a small part of St Giles Community Centre. This Centre was amply provided with a main hall, modern kitchen, gymnasium and numerous meeting rooms. A cupboard in the kitchen was used to store food collected as supermarket surplus from Sainsbury's,

Tesco, ASDA and M&S. Canterbury's, a smaller independent supermarket chain, also contributed generously.

The St. Giles Mini Food Supply Hub was open every Wednesday afternoon where bags of supermarket surplus food had been made up to be collected by needy families. There was no strict means test used to ascertain who was entitled to take advantage of this facility but it was generally expected that those who benefitted had children in receipt of free school meals or who were on universal credit. There were a number of families who, for one very good reason or another, were unable to visit St. Giles to collect food bags and Marion's team of volunteers would personally deliver bags to these homes. No charge was made to those being served by the mini food supply hub.

During school holidays, the mini food supply hub served hot meals between 12 noon and 2:00 pm to families who had come to collect food bags during term time. These lunches were prepared by members of Marion's team whose culinary skills were up to cooking for large numbers. Those members of the team whose time was not fully occupied in the cooking and serving of these meals would join individual families at the tables where they were eating and get into conversation with these families to get to know them better and appreciate their needs. Where appropriate, they would share their faith with these families as very few of them had any meaningful connection with church.

Christine and Michael were included in the team which supported Marion in the mini food supply hub initiative. Work commitments meant that they were seldom available to help on Wednesday afternoons. However, when off duty, Christine and Michael were able to collect carloads of the surplus food from the supermarkets. They formed excellent relationships with the managers and staff of these supermarkets. In particular, they found Jeremy Kimber, the manager of Canterbury's, a store in a small independent supermarket chain, to be most helpful.

One day when Christine called at Canterbury's to collect food, she thought that Jeremy looked particularly worried and preoccupied and she asked Jeremy if he was facing any particular problem. He invited Christine into his office where he explained the problem.

"Like all the main supermarket chains, we have saved a lot of money in staffing by setting up self-checkout tills," he started, "but our savings are being reduced by what I believe to be an increased level of shop-lifting.

I think that self-checkouts lend themselves to shoplifting in a way which wasn't possible when customers wheeled their trolleys through a normal, staff-operated checkout. People probably believe that cheating a machine is fair game but there is no such thing as a victimless crime. The more money we lose through shoplifting, the less our profits and the higher the prices we have to charge so everyone loses out."

"How do shoplifters operate in the self-checkout areas?" asked Christine. "I have occasionally been embarrassed myself when a voice at the station where I have been checking out declares that *there's an unexpected item in the bagging area!*' when the item I thought I had scanned hadn't properly registered. The system seems pretty fool proof"

"Yes," said Jeremy, "if people scan one item at a time there is no problem but if two items are put into a bag together and only one has been scanned, the system won't necessarily realise this. The staff on duty should spot when this sort of thing is being done but they can't keep their eyes simultaneously trained on twelve checkouts, especially when distracted by the need to help another customer who is having difficulty with the checkout system. The bigger supermarket chains may have solved this problem but Canterbury's self-checkout system may need some attention."

Jeremy took Christine for a stroll by the self-checkout area where a vigilant member of staff was paying close attention to what the customers were doing. Everything seemed to be under control but the shop's accounting system indicated that the level of shoplifting was too high.

Christine said that this was not just a supermarket problem but all crime is a matter of concern for the police. She would give some thought as to how improvements might be put into place. Within two days, Christine had some ideas and came back to discuss them with Jeremy.

"What information is accessible when the barcode of an item is scanned at the checkout?" asked Christine.

"Merely the name of the item and its price," replied Jeremy. "As the item is scanned, the computer registers this name and the price. A cumulative total price is calculated by the computer and all this appears at the end of the printout listing purchases as payment is made."

"How accurate are the scales used to weigh the bags at checkout?" asked Christine.
"They're very good. I've been told that they are accurate to + or − 10 grams," he replied.

"Then the accuracy of these scales could be exploited to good effect," continued Christine. "As it is now, customers place the items they have taken from the shelves directly into their trolley or basket. I would suggest that as customers enter the supermarket with their trolley, a member of staff gives them specially shaped bags which exactly line the wire trolley, two bags for the larger trolleys but one should be sufficient for the smaller trolleys. The weight of every item on the supermarket shelves as well as the names of items and prices needs to be included on the database which stores all the necessary information about the items on sale. On entering the self-checkout area, the customer should place a bag full of shopping on to a scale-pan to the right of the scanner. As an item is taken out of a bag, the change in weight will be registered on the computer system used to control and monitor the self-checkout area. The computer should be programmed to compare this weight with the item's weight stored in the computer's database which will be revealed as the barcode is scanned. The two weights should match and should be the same as that which becomes registered as the item is placed in the customer's bag on a scale pan in the bagging area to the left of the scanning table. If correctly used, all three weights should be the same within the + or - 10 gram tolerance which represents the limit of accuracy of the scales."

"This sounds good," enthused Jeremy. "It certainly overcomes the problem of multiple items being transferred to the customer's bag without each one being individually scanned. Updating the data base with the item's weight will be a time-consuming but one-off job. An additional scale will be required at each self-checkout station but this again is a one-off investment. A large number of specially shaped bags will need to be made to line the shopping trolleys but these should have many weeks, if not months, of life."

"I know that you have closed circuit TV cameras placed at strategic points around the shop," said Christine. "I imagine you have members of staff in a room somewhere, observing the associated screens."

"Of course," said Jeremy Kimber.

"Then, if any extra security is needed in the self-checkout area," continued Christine, "I would suggest that you place a set of security cameras above the self-checkout stations. They can be mounted quite high up so as not to be obvious to the customers. I would estimate that each camera could take in three checkout stations. It would probably be easier for any inappropriate action being carried out by a customer to be observed on these monitors rather than by the member of staff supervising the area at ground level, in view of all the distractions to which they're subject."

"I'm amazed at the ideas you've come up with in so short a time," enthused Jeremy as he accompanied Christine out of Canterbury's. "I'll be in touch with head office to sound out their reaction and will keep you informed."

Christine was able to let the mini food supply hub team know about her visit to Canterbury's when they met later in the week. Another member of the team, Sydney Kenyon, raised another matter. Sydney was the greatly loved churchwarden. He was grey-haired, upright and sprightly but it was difficult to estimate his age which could have been anything between fifty and seventy.

"When we're sharing meals with the families during holiday times," Sydney started, "we've recognised that this provides an opportunity to share our faith. However, I've been very unsuccessful at doing this. The families aren't interested and they invariably steer any promising conversation off into an unhelpful direction."
"I suspect that you have some ideas on how we can be more successful in this direction," interjected Marion who was chairing the meeting.

"I think that a pair of us working together and following a pre-arranged script might work," Sydney suggested.

The group continued by discussing such strategies before praying over this issue. Sydney and Michael, working together, were indeed able to put this strategy into good effect, the next time they shared a meal put on by the mini food supply hub during the school holidays.

Returning to the encounter described earlier in this chapter between Christine and Jeremy Kimber, the manager of Canterbury's Supermarket, Christine was delighted to hear a few days later that Mr. Jeremy Kimber had been warmly congratulated and commended by Canterbury's top management on the ideas he had shared. Although he had declared that these had been the brainchild of a police officer friend rather than his own, Jeremy was still given credit for drawing the management's attention to this idea. They were seriously looking into the feasibility of installing the system Christine had suggested in the self-checkout areas in the small chain of Canterbury's supermarkets and this would be piloted at the Oakenhampton branch.

Chapter 6

<u>The Services of a Vet and Food Bank Needed</u>

Christine and Bill were on the early shift, walking along Oakenhampton High Street in the opposite direction to the children on their way to school. They particularly noticed a boy of about ten and a somewhat younger girl who was crying as they plodded along. Christine stopped to ask what was wrong. They had some hesitation before replying so Christine showed them her warrant card and explained they were plain clothes police officers who were always ready to step in and help if they thought there was a problem.

The children were brother and sister, Stuart and Jennifer Boyd.

"Mum told us this morning that we were going to have to get rid of our dog," Jennifer explained, "because we can't afford to feed him and pay the vet's bill now that he seems to be unwell."

"We're very poor," Stuart added, "and I'm worried that Mum isn't feeding herself properly although she makes sure that we always have enough."

"Well," said Christine, "That's something we really should be able to help you with. I'll call round with a friend who knows about dogs this evening and tell your mother about the food bank where I help out. Let me know your address and I'll visit your Mum tonight."

That evening, Christine, accompanied by Michael arrived at a small semi-detached house located in a crescent just off the High Street at the far end of Oakenhampton.

The children had obviously told their mother about the policewoman they had met that morning because Christine could see that they were not unexpected when a slightly built woman in her early forties answered the door. She wore a cardigan with a delicate Fair Isle pattern. Christine guessed that she had knitted this herself. Her hair was slightly greying but neatly combed and tied back. Although her face was thin, Mrs. Boyd wore a genuinely kind expression. Christine showed her her warrant card by way of introduction and introduced Michael as a vet. They were ushered into a sparsely furnished living room. Mrs Boyd asked if they would like a drink, tea or coffee? Yes, a cup of instant coffee would be fine, both with milk and no sugar. Christine and Michael took their seats and Mrs Boyd went out to return a few minutes later with a tray bearing coffees and a plate of biscuits.

Mrs. Boyd explained that the children were in their bedrooms, Jennifer playing computer games on her laptop and Stuart, getting on with his homework for which he also needed a laptop.

"Your children tell me that they're worried that you're not eating as well as they think you should," started Christine which partly explained why she had come round that evening. "Well, I help out at a type of food bank at St Giles church and we're there for the very purpose of helping the many people like yourself who've been hit by this unprecedented rise in the cost of living."

Mrs. Boyd explained their situation :-
"We were able to cope fairly well when my husband was alive but sadly, he died of Covid six months ago. I didn't think people died from the recent variants of Covid as they did a couple of years ago when the pandemic first broke but Leonard had a weak chest, he suffered from bronchitis. He spent ten days in the intensive care unit and had the best attention possible but sadly the medics couldn't save him. Well, since then, it's been very difficult to make both ends meet. The children have needed new clothes and although I can get most clothes second hand or from charity shops, I refuse to get their shoes from anywhere but a proper shoe shop. Children's feet can be permanently

damaged by ill fitting shoes and you can only be sure of getting the right shoes when their feet are properly measured at a shoe shop. It's hard to believe how expensive good quality shoes are now, even for children.

I'm afraid I wouldn't qualify to receive anything from your food bank because I have a part time job and I'm not on Universal Credit. I just about get by if I restrict my food shopping to ASDA basics. The dog is almost as expensive to feed as the children. They were so upset when I suggested that we might have to get rid of him that I don't really think that I can. However, I think the dog is going to need veterinary attention. I haven't got a pet insurance and I just won't be able to afford the vet bills."

"You should certainly come to our food bank which we call a mini food supply hub because it doesn't run in quite the same way as a conventional food bank" said Christine. "We don't have any enrolment criteria. We're there to meet genuine need and from what Stuart and Jennifer have told us and indeed, from the way you have described your situation, we think that a genuine need does exist here. Do come along on Wednesday afternoon when we're open. There's not a large choice of foodstuffs as we're dependent on what the supermarkets regard as surplus and which are near their sell-by date. Supermarkets err well on the side of safety in setting their sell-by dates. Items labelled 'best before' can be safely consumed well after the date listed on the packaging. We pack a good range of foodstuffs into bags and there is always extra for families with children."

"That's so kind of you," beamed Mrs. Boyd, realising that this could take pressure off her very tight budget. "My main problem is in paying my energy bills. They warned us that our bills could go up by a factor of three but I'm now paying six times what I was paying this time last year! I'm paying £200 a month for 'supply maintenance' and I don't know what this means. I have complained to my energy supplier but they say that they are only charging me the price they have to in view of the global rise in the price of fuel."

"Who is your energy supplier?" asked Christine.

"Jouleserve," replied Mrs. Boyd.

"How do you pay your fuel bills?" asked Christine.

"I pay all my utility bills by direct debit. This guarantees that I won't get into debt by missing a payment, provided that I make sure that the money is there in the bank."

Christine paused to think for a moment. She'd never heard of energy companies charging for 'supply maintenance'.

"This may seem an awful cheek, but could I see the receipts you are getting for your energy payments," asked Christine.

"Certainly," replied Mrs. Boyd. "The main supply of energy is broken down into a receipt for gas and a separate one for electricity. The 'supply maintenance' is receipted separately."

Mrs. Boyd went out into another room to find the receipts leaving Christine and Michael looking rather puzzled. Michael hadn't heard of 'supply maintenance' either.

A short time later, Mrs. Boyd came back with a bundle of papers and handed them to Christine. The gas and electricity receipts looked in order. The 'supply maintenance' receipt had the same 'Jouleserve' heading except that a different address was listed. The address looked like a private house in Oakenhampton rather than a location on an industrial estate.

"Direct debits like those shown on the energy supply receipts usually vary from month to month. However, the 'supply maintenance' receipt is always for exactly £200," observed Christine. "This may seem an even more outrageous thing to ask, but could you let me see your bank statement?"

By now, Christine, as a fairly senior police officer, had built up a relationship of trust between herself and Mrs Boyd and without hesitation, she went out to retrieve her bank statements. She returned and handed Christine a file with an embossed heading, 'Chiltern and Cotswold' Bank'. Christine browsed through the statements.

"I thought you said you paid your utility bills by direct debit but I see you pay for your 'supply maintenance' by standing order." observed Christine.

"No," said Mrs Boyd, "The only payments I make by standing order are to two charities, the British Red Cross and Global Care, a Christian charity. I sponsor a child supported by this charity. Sadly, the way my finances are going at present, I may have to cancel these standing orders."

Christine handed the bank statement to Mrs. Boyd and pointed out where the payment to 'Jouleserve Supply Maintenance' was paid by standing order.

Mrs. Boyd scrutinised the statement with a puzzled expression.

"I never authorised such a payment," she declared, "and neither would my husband have done when he was alive. He couldn't cope with online banking and so I dealt with all bank transactions."

"I suspect some hacker has somehow managed to take control of your bank account," said Christine. "I'll need to make some enquiries at your bank. Also, it would be very useful if I could get our Cyber Crime forensic team to look at your computer. I think that a serious crime has taken place here. Are you prepared to let me borrow your computer to have it investigated? Would 'not having access' to your computer seriously inconvenience you?"

"No," said Mrs. Boyd. "we had to get laptops for the children during the pandemic as these were needed to enable them to cope with their schoolwork. The main thing I use the computer for is online shopping and I can do that perfectly well on one of the children's laptops. No, please take the computer and do any tests that are needed. This needs to be cleared up as quickly as possible."

Mrs. Boyd went out and returned, this time bearing a slim Dell laptop which she handed to Christine.

"In order to make enquiries at your bank, I'll need you to give authorisation, either in writing or by phone," explained Christine. "The bank won't allow me to see your bank account without a warrant unless I have your express permission."

"I'll see to that first thing in the morning," said Mrs. Boyd, obviously anxious to get this matter cleared up as soon as possible.

Michael, who had been silent for most of this time, then spoke.

"Christine told you I was a vet when she introduced me. I would like to see your dog. I may be able to help out there."

Michael noticed a worried look come over Mrs Boyd's face.

"Don't worry," he continued, "I'm not going to charge you exorbitant vet fees."

Mrs. Boyd went to the door but this time she didn't go out. She just called in a high voice, "Pixie!"

A lovely but lethargic looking cockerpoo waddled in. Michael held out his hand and the dog made his way over. Michael stroked Pixie and then lifted him on to his lap and examined him.

"I don't think there is anything seriously wrong with Pixie that can't be cleared up with a few tablets which I can drop round tomorrow," he said. "Where did you buy the dog?"

"They were advertised at a very reasonable price by someone living in Simbourne. I'll look up the address."

Mrs. Boyd went out again and returned this time with an address she had neatly written on a piece of paper and handed this to Michael. Simbourne was a Cotswold village not far from Oakenhampton.

That completed the business and Christine and Michael had come to talk about and they got up to leave.

"We'll keep you in touch with any developments," promised Christine as they were shown to the front door, Christine clutching the laptop under her arm.

"That was an interesting meeting," said Christine once they were out of earshot of the house. "Clearly, there are limes of enquiry must be followed up in view of what Mrs. Boyd has told us."

"Yes," agreed Michael, "and I would like to visit the place where Mrs Boyd bought that dog. Several people have come into the vets with cockerpoos in a poor state and they were all bought from Simbourne. Would you be prepared to come there with me tomorrow evening? I'll get my friend, Richard Carstairs to join us. He's an RSPCA inspector."

"Certainly," replied Christine.

Chapter 7

<u>Fruitful Lines of Enquiry</u>

The first thing that Christine did on arriving at the police station the following morning was to let Chief Inspector Whittaker's secretary know that she was uncovering what appeared to be a serious crime. She asked the secretary to let her know as soon as the Chief Inspector came in so that she could update him. The Superintendent arrived at 10:00 am and phoned down for Christine to come up.

Without going into the foodbank arrangement or the proposed visit to Simbourne where possibly, dogs were being bred and sold illegally, Christine explained very carefully how it appeared that Mrs Boyd's computer might well have been hacked, costing her a considerable amount of money. She asked if it could be arranged for the Cyber Crime Team to have a look at the computer. Chief Inspector Whittaker immediately appreciated that this was a serious matter and agreed that the Cyber Crime Team should be contacted to investigate. An hour later, a member of the Team arrived at Oakenhampton police station and collected Mrs. Boyd's laptop from Christine.

Christine, accompanied by Bill, then made her way to the local branch of the Chiltern and Cotswold Bank and asked to see the manager. Christine had brought Bill up to date with the visit to Mrs Boyd the previous evening. They were not unexpected. Mr Padbury, the manager, had already received a call from Mrs. Boyd to let him know that the police wished to have access to her bank account. The last thing bank managers want is the discovery of irregular dealings in the way accounts are managed. Christine and Bill were shown into Mr. Padbury's office. He greeted them most courteously and arranged for coffee and biscuits to be served. This time, the beverage was a high quality Brazilian percolated coffee.

Christine got down to business straight away and enquired about payments made by standing order to the Jouleserve Supply Maintenance account. Who had set this up and why did it operate from a different address from the main Jouleserve Energy Supply address? Mr Padbury couldn't explain this but stated that the account had been set up by the chairman and company secretary of 'Jouleserve Supply Maintenance' which was a subsidiary of 'Jouleserve Energy Supply'. The paperwork all seemed to be in order and a small bank like the Chiltern and Cotswold Bank welcomed having the custom of a major energy supplier. Mr Padbury had sent up to them, the forms which had been completed when the account had been set up. Yes, they were duly signed by the chairman and company secretary but professionals with high status seem to delight in using illegible signatures. Christine asked for a photocopy of this document.

She then asked Mr Padbury how a standing order could be set up without the account holder knowing.

"Impossible," said Mr Padbury. "Whenever a transaction like this is made, a one-time identification code is sent to the account holder's mobile phone to ensure that it is indeed the account holder making the transaction. The account holder making the transaction has to enter this identification code before the transaction can be completed."

This left Christine and Bill severely puzzled. Mrs Boyd would have certainly known that she had done this if she had indeed set up the standing order.

Christine asked Mr Padbury how many clients paid Jouleserve Supply Maintenance by standing order.

Mr. Padbury phoned down to a bank clerk to look this up and after a few moments the clerk rang back to give him this information. Twenty-five clients paid £200 a month by standing order. Mr. Padbury was reluctant to let Christine and Bill know the names of these clients without a special warrant.

Christine asked "What happens to the money which accumulates in the Jouleserve Supply Maintenance account?

"It doesn't accumulate there," Mr Padbury explained. "Every month, it's paid into an account in a bank in the Cayman Islands."

'Money laundering' was the thought that went through everyone's mind.

Christine came away from the bank feeling quite worried. At this stage, it seemed unlikely that they could get the warrant they needed to identify the clients who were paying 'Jouleserve Supply Maintenance' by standing order. Bill however was upbeat. He was fairly confident that the Cyber Crime Team would come up with some answers. Being very much a lateral thinker, Bill was also the first one to connect this crime with Hamish McIntosh's murder.

"I think that we should look at the client list we found on Hamish McIntosh's laptop. I've a hunch we'll find a connection."

That afternoon, they trawled through the information on the list of names which Christine had printed out from Hamish's computer. These included their addresses, bank account details, phone numbers and computer identities. Some entries had been highlighted. These were all individuals who held bank accounts at the Chiltern and Cotswold Bank and yes, Mrs Boyd's details were there. This was indeed a significant discovery.

Later that afternoon, Christine and Bill called at the address on the header of the 'Jouleserve Supply Maintenance' receipts which they had noted when they visited Mrs. Boyd. They arrived at a small house in a crescent just off the High Street on the outskirts of Oakenhampton. There was mutual surprise when the door was opened by Olivia Clark, the admin assistant at C & E Software Enterprises. Olivia invited them in.

Christine immediately got down to business and showed Olivia the receipts.

"We've come to enquire why these receipts from 'Jouleserve Supply Maintenance' should bear your address?"

"This is something that Henry and Courtney have arranged. They told me that they are doing a job for

'Jouleserve Supply Maintenance' which requires correspondence to be sent out in their name but handled by ourselves. Every month, they give me a list of names to whom I send out receipts and occasionally, mail arrives here addressed to 'Jouleserve Supply Maintenance'."

"Yes," asked Christine, "but why use your address? Why can't this mail be directed to your office at C & E Software Enterprises?"

"Henry and Courtney told me that when the janitor comes in every morning, he sorts out all the letters which are addressed to the various firms which occupy offices in our building. He would just return the ones addressed to 'Jouleserve Supply Maintenance' as unknown at this address," explained Olivia. "As more than one janitor is employed at the building, Henry and Courtney considered it safer to have this correspondence delivered here rather than go astray through misdirection. They told me that the contents are sensitive and they asked me not to open these letters as they arrive, but just to bring them to the office when I come into work."

This explanation indicated to Christine and Bill that Henry and Courtney were clearly involved in the standing order scam and realised that Olivia would not be able to enlighten them any further. They thanked Olivia and left her house. It was now quite late in the day.

"We're going to need to call at C & E Software Enterprises first thing tomorrow morning," stated Christine to Bill. "How ever did you come to suspect that this crime might be connected to the Hamish murder?"

"When I looked carefully at the fairly illegible signatures on the form used to open the account at the Chiltern and Cotswold Bank, I could see that the names scrawled were possibly H. R. Erikson and C. Cavendish."

"Well spotted, Bill."

Chapter 8

<u>The Illegal Puppy Farm</u>

That evening, Christine and Michael, together with his friend Richard who was an RSPCA inspector, made their way to the address where Mrs. Boyd had bought her puppy. They arrived at Simbourne and located the house in a quiet street off the main road. They called at the door which was answered by a rather surly individual wearing a vest but no shirt. He looked them up and down. He barked a single word.

"Yes!"

"We gather that you are in the business of selling puppies," started Michael. "Do you have a licence to run a puppy farm?"

"I don't run a puppy farm. I just sell the puppies which my pet bitch whelps," replied the man.

From the number of dogs Michael had seen, he realised that more than one bitch was involved.

"Well," continued Michael, "I'm a vet and from the number of dogs which have been brought to me which you supplied, I imagine your dog must be breaking world records.”

Michael hadn’t seen that many dogs but he had a hunch the man was lying.

“Can I see your dog?”

“No!”

Christine then stepped in and showed her warrant card.

“We can come here again with a search warrant but I’m sure that you wouldn’t want your neighbours to see your house swarming with uniformed police officers. If you’ve nothing to hide, why not just let us see your dog?”

The man hesitated for a moment.

“All right then, follow me.”

“He led them round to the back of the house where there were three fairly large pens, each housing a dog and two or three puppies. The place was not as bad as some of the illegal puppy farms which have been shown on the television The pens were of adequate size. There was clean straw on the ground. The kennels were robust and waterproof. The dogs were obviously well fed and there was water in each pen. However, things were not as good as they should have been. Dog faeces had not been cleared from the pens and the water in the bowls needed to be changed.

"This is clearly a puppy farm," said Richard. "I've seen a lot worse but things here are not as good as they should be. You need to get yourself licenced with the Kennel Club who will inspect the premises and show you what must be done to get it up to scratch. You may have to take a test to satisfy them that you are aware of how caring for dogs and dog breeding should be carried out and they can give you training if that's needed. Get yourself registered. We will be back in a week or so's time to check that all this has been put in hand."

The man led them back to the front of the house.

"I didn't know that you had to be registered, just to sell a few puppies."

"You do if you are doing this on a commercial scale. Having three pens to keep your dogs in shows that these are not just domestic pets." stated Richard.

"Ignorance of the law is not accepted as a defence if you should ever have to defend yourself in court," added Christine, "but now you know the odds so there's no reason why you shouldn't get your act together and breed your dogs in the best possible environment."

The man said a grudging 'good bye' as they left the premises.

"That visit was well worthwhile," said Richard, the RSPCA inspector. "Thank you both for alerting my attention to this illegal puppy farm. Puppies are often born into much worse conditions than what we've just seen but that's no reason why anyone profiting from the sale of animals like this man is, shouldn't provide them with the very best environment. I'm sure that when I visit the premises again, I'll find everything much improved."

With that, the three of them returned to Oakenhampton.

Chapter 9

<u>The Deserted Office</u>

First thing the following morning, Christine and Bill arrived at the C & E Software Enterprises office and they were met by a very distressed Olivia.

"When I arrived this morning," she wept, "I found the office had been cleared out. The wastepaper baskets were full of shredded paper, the computers were gone and the cupboards empty. I found money on my desk which was equivalent to a month's wages and I assume that that has been left for me in lieu of notice. I have tried to contact Henry and Courtney by phone but their phones aren't responding. I don't know what to do."

"I can see you're upset and I can understand why," sympathised Christine, "but I can assure you that you're well clear of Henry and Courtney The best thing you can do is to take the money and start looking for another job. We'll doubtless be getting in touch with you again but if you can think of anything else which might help us find Henry and Courtney please get in touch."

Christine gave Olivia a card with the contact details of Oakenhampton police station.

"Did you tell Henry and Courtney that we'd called on you yesterday?" asked Bill.

"Well, yes," responded Olivia. "They are, no, they were my employers and it seemed the right thing to do. I didn't know that they would up sticks and away on hearing that the police were making enquiries."

"Although it seems that they have disconnected their phones, could you let me have their numbers and any other numbers they might contact," asked Christine.

Olivia rummaged through the drawer in her desk which Henry and Courtney. had not disturbed when they cleared the office. She came out with an A4 sheet listing about twenty phone numbers.

Christine studied the sheet. Most were the sort of numbers you might expect an IT firm to have on file, - PC World, Dell Computers, Cartridge Save, Hewlett Packard and so on. Two numbers stood out as different.

"Who are Eleanor Pedlingham and Elizabeth Draycott?" she asked.

"They're Henry and Courtney's girlfriends," explained Olivia. "They often phone them from the office and occasionally, these ladies phone here. They have visited the office. They're very smart. I wish I could afford their clothes."

By now, Olivia had calmed down. Christine and Bill sympathised with Olivia for the shock they realised that this had been to her. They asked her for Henry and Courtney's addresses and reminded her to keep in touch if anything came up.

Christine and Bill called at the addresses which Olivia had given them They were up-market apartments in neighbouring Cotswold villages. There were no replies when they rang at these apartments. With help from neighbours, they were able to locate the landlord. He was prepared to allow access to the apartments to two police officers in view of the seriousness of the crime they were investigating even though, at the time, they hadn't obtained a search warrant. As speed in contacting Courtney and Henry seemed essential, Christine and Bill had come straight to these addresses on leaving Olivia at the C & E Software Enterprises office.

On entering these apartments, Christine and Bill found signs that the occupants had obviously left in a hurry. There were no clothes in the drawers or cupboards which had been left open and nothing that could be described as a personal possession. They then returned to Oakenhampton police station to report to the Chief Inspector.

On being brought up to date, Chief Inspector Colin Whittaker immediately arranged for the numbers of Henry and Courtney's cars to be included on the police patrol cars' on-board computers as vehicles of interest. Remembering how useful the mobile phone numbers had been in tracking down the people involved in human trafficking, Christine suggested that the phones of Eleanor Pedlingham and Elizabeth Draycott should be similarly monitored.

"This can only be arranged in the most serious of cases," Chief Inspector Colin Whittaker explained. "The evidence picked up on these is of limited value in court. However, people trafficking is a crime which is given very high priority. The disappearance of two people from their place of work may not be regarded as so important."

"The disappearance of Henry and Courtney may be just one line of enquiry in a murder investigation but there aren't many crimes as serious as murder. I consider Henry and Courtney to be prime suspects and deserving the fullest attention of the police in order to get them apprehended," protested Christine.

"You're quite right," replied Colin, "I'll arrange for the phones of Eleanor Pedlingham and Elizabeth Draycott to be monitored but it may take some time."

Chapter 10

<u>Closing the Net</u>

"Two days later, a very significant development occurred. A member of the Cyber Crime team, Inspector George Apsley, arrived at the Oakenhampton police station to meet with Colin, Christine and Bill. He was carrying Mrs Boyd's computer.

"It would appear that this computer had been hacked," he explained. "There's a trojan which is concealed on a web site which appears among the news and information on Microsoft Network homepage. As you know, a trojan is a virus concealed within another programme or piece of software, ostensibly designed for a completely different purpose. Microsoft aren't as careful as they might be in vetting material they allow to be put on this homepage. We've already investigated this site in connection with another complaint. The viewer is offered a prize of £100 if they can correctly answer ten questions on moderately obscure facts in history within ten minutes. The offer of a prize leads many people to log onto this website. Once logged on, the trojan allows a remote user to take control of the computer. Having established control, there's no limit to the damage which the remote user might inflict. In this case, it seems that the hacker was concerned with getting into the computer's on-line banking app. You'd be surprised at how many people keep their passwords in an easily accessible file, even one labelled 'Passwords'. Some people have as their password for all applications just the single word, 'password'! This makes it all too easy for the hacker. With the password, the hacker can get into the user's bank account although banks have taken steps to make unauthorised paying out money from accounts difficult.

We've been able to look at the recent transactions on Mrs Boyd's computer, and it would appear that on entering her online banking app, the mobile phone number was changed. A four-digit number was then entered and the hacker was able to authorise a standing order of £200 a month to another account held by the Chiltern and Cotswold Bank. Having completed this transaction, the hacker changed the mobile phone number back to the original number and logged out. The change of the mobile phone number in the user's personal details enables the hacker to access the one-time authorisation code needed to carry out transactions on the banking app. All this can be done in the space of a very few minutes and as it appears that this work was done during the night, the computer owner would be none the wiser until they discovered they were paying out an unauthorised £200 every month."

"That is a very useful development," said Colin as he thanked Inspector George Apsley who had brought in the information. He phoned down for coffee and they continued to chat.

"I'm very interested in this history quiz which people are tempted to enter with the lure of £100 prize," Colin said. "What sort of questions are asked? I wonder if any of us could answer them?"

The Inspector George took out a sheet from his brief case and passed in round.

"Here are the questions."

1. What injury did Lord Uxbridge, Wellington's second in command, sustain in the Battle of Waterloo?

2. What was the name of the tribe led by Boadicea when she fought against the Romans?

3. How many of Henry VIII's wives died from complications arising during childbirth?

4. What was the name of Admiral Collingwood's ship at the battle of Trafalgar?

5. How did Clive of India die?

6. What was the first big battle fought in 1066 to prevent England from being invaded by a foreign power?

7. Who was England's youngest Prime Minister?

8. Westminster Abbey was founded by Edward the Confessor but in which king's reign was it rebuilt?

9. Why is King's College, Cambridge written with an apostrophe before the s but Queens' College written with an apostrophe after the s?

10. What leisure time activity did Hitler and Churchill have in common?

Answers

1. He lost a leg
2. Iceni
3. Two, Jane Seymour and Catherine Parr.
4. The Royal Sovereign
5. He committed suicide.
6. Stamford Bridge
7. William Pitt, the Younger (Prime Minister at age 24)
8. Henry III
9. King's College was founded by Henry VI but Queens' College was founded by two queens, first, Margaret of Anjou, Henry VI's wife and then re-founded by her Yorkist rival, Elizabeth Woodville.
10. They both enjoyed painting.

"I don't think I could do many of those," confessed Christine.

The others agreed that they all looked difficult.

"Well," Inspector George Apsley continued, "the lure of the £100 prize lured many into accessing this quiz and badly infecting their computers in the process. The hackers obviously thought they were pretty safe from having to hand out a prize because the second question is a catch. Two of Henry VIII's wives died as a result of childbirth, Jane Seymour and also his last wife, Catherine Parr. However, Catherine's child was not fathered by Henry VIII but by her fourth husband, Thomas Seymour, whom she married after Henry VIII died."

"Can we positively identify the hacker who carried out this deceit," asked Colin.

"That's something we're working on," replied George, "but these cyber criminals are very clever at covering their tracks so we've had no luck in that direction so far."

Colin, Christine and Bill thanked Inspector George for his valuable contribution to their on-going investigation and he headed back to the Cyber Crime Investigation headquarters.

The following day, Superintendent Whittaker was able to report to Christine and Bill that the Met had approved creating clones to Eleanor Pedlingham and Elizabeth Draycott's phones.

"Their calls will be continuously monitored and there is a good chance that Henry Erikson or Courtney

Cavendish will contact one or the other at some point." he reported.

Several days went by with no news from that quarter and neither had the cars bearing the number plates that Christine had noted been spotted by a patrol car. Then a breakthrough suddenly occurred. The phone calls which had been monitored up to that point had been largely conversations between Elizabeth and Eleanor with their friends and family but at last, the awaited call came up on Elizabeth's phone. A transcript of the conversation was as follows.

> Henry:- Hallo Elizabeth. I'm sorry that I've been so long in getting in touch. A problem has come up which Courtney and I think has put us in danger and we've been lying low.

> Elizabeth:- Whatever's this problem? It must be pretty serious. Eleanor and I have been worried sick about you and Courtney.

> Henry:- It's too complicated to explain and I don't think we'll ever be able to explain it without causing you and Eleanor even more worry.

Look, I was really phoning to see if we could meet up as a foursome again in the very near future?

Elizabeth:- Well, that would be nice. When and where do you suggest?

Henry:- The Snow Leopard in Beaconsfield, Wednesday night at 7:00 pm

Elizabeth:- That's a bit of a long way for us to go for an evening out and the Snow Leopard is quite an expensive place to eat out at.

Henry:- Beaconsfield is a good halfway point between your part of London and the Cotswolds and its easily accessible from the M40. Don't worry about the cost. As usual, Courtney and I will pay the bill

Elizabeth:- Well, yes, If you're paying, I'm free. I'll get in touch with Eleanor to make sure that she can come too.

Henry:- There should be no need for you to do that. Courtney will be contacting her himself.

Elizabeth:- I look forward to Wednesday then.

Henry:- Must ring off now. We'll catch up on
news on Wednesday.

A similar phone call had been monitored between
Courtney and Eleanor.

As soon as Colin had received this news, he called in
Christine and Bill to put them in the picture.

"We'll arrange for two plain clothes officers to be
sitting at a table near the one that Henry and Courtney
have booked. Obviously, it can't be either of you
because you'd be recognised. We'll have a back-up
team waiting in cars in the restaurant carpark. I'll put
the restaurant manager in the picture about what will be
going on. Although you won't be sitting in the
restaurant when the foursome are all together, it should
be possible to arrange for you two to be the arresting
officers. You deserve that after all the work you've
done on this case."

Christine and Bill left the meeting with Colin in a state
of some euphoria.

Chapter 11

<u>Unsuitable Marriage Partners</u>

Two women were sitting at a corner table in a branch of Café Nero, not too far from the Houses of Parliament. They were strikingly attractive. Elizabeth Draycott was wearing a well-fitting, knee length, powder blue coat. Her companion, Eleanor Pedlingham, wore a smartly tailored, camel coloured skirt suit. They were wearing the ubiquitous patent leather high heeled shoes which young women regard as necessary footwear if they're to be seen as fashionably attired. Elizabeth was blond while Eleanor's hair was auburn. Both women wore stylish coiffures. They each sported the most beautiful brooches on the lapels of their coats which glistened in the light in a way which left one believing that they must be set with real diamonds, emeralds, sapphires and rubies, but if so, these brooches must have been worth well over a thousand pounds, if not several thousand. With such flawless complexions, little makeup was required to enhance the well contoured features of Elizabeth and Eleanor's delightful faces. Even the Princess of Wales would have had to be at her best to rival the appearance of these lovely ladies. Were they models working for Dior or Yves St. Laurent? No, they were administrative grade civil servants. Elizabeth worked for the Home Office while Eleanor ran a department in the Treasury. Elizabeth and Eleanor had been great friends since studying at Newnham College, Cambridge. Elizabeth had studied Life Sciences while Eleanor had read Economics. Both had graduated with good degrees and passed their Civil Service entrance exams with flying colours.

Elizabeth sipped her flat white while Eleanor stirred her mocha. What do single women talk about over coffee during their break times? They were discussing the merits of their current boyfriends. They had met them at an expensive dating agency after their previous relationships had been terminated by mutual consent. The dating agency had arranged for the prospective partners to sit in pairs at well separated tables where they had just over a quarter of an hour to talk and get to know as much as they could about each other during this limited time span. A buzzer was sounded at the end of the quarter hour and the men moved on to the next table while the ladies remained seated at the same table. Food and drink was served during the three hours that the meetings had taken place. At the end of the evening, they had all departed with a list of the names and addresses of the ten persons they had met during the session. The idea was that they could communicate in their own time with any on their list whom they would like to meet on a date, but there was no obligation to accept the offer of the date.

Not unsurprisingly, Elizabeth and Eleanor were invited to date all ten of the men they had met at the agency but only two had really stood out as special, Henry Erikson and Courtney Cavendish. In consultation with each other, Elizabeth and Eleanor made their choice to avoid dating the same man. Elizabeth dated Henry while Eleanor chose Courtney. In view of the fact that Henry and Courtney had handsome appearances, swagger and charm which the other eight men lacked, it is perhaps surprising that only five of the women at the dating agency had contacted Henry and Courtney but some women claim to have an infallible instinct in deciding on the suitability of men friends. Elizabeth and Eleanor had now been seeing Eric and Courtney for the best part of ten months, mostly in pairs but occasionally as a foursome. These took place after the time when they had all attended a party given by Janice, a mutual university friend of Elizabeth and Eleanor. The guests had been invited to attend with their partners.

"How are things going with Courtney?" asked Elizabeth.

"When we first went out, I felt, Bingo! this is the man for me. He was self-assured, charming and witty and I found him to be good company. However, as I've got to know him better, my enthusiasm for Courtney has cooled. I'm very wary about falling in love with a man who shows no sign of falling in love with me and in spite of his apparently friendly disposition, I feel that Courtney is keeping me at arm's length. He doesn't really seem interested in the work I do or my hobbies. He won't come to church with me and I don't think he realised that you and I knew each other before attending that dating agency until we all attended Janice's party! Courtney is very full of himself, his achievements, his cleverness and his status as director of a small firm. Although he invariably greets me with the words. "You look great," it never goes beyond that. He's never hinted that he is even beginning to love me. I've received neither a birthday nor a Valentine card from him but he has given me a very expensive gift as Henry has to you."

Eleanor was referring to the jewelled brooches they both wore.

"I'm glad you've told me this, Eleanor, because I'm feeling much the same way about Henry. Yes, they're both very wealthy and so, although of great intrinsic value to ourselves, I don't suppose our brooches made a great hole in Henry and Courtney's pockets. But a person's wealth is the last attribute one should consider when deciding whether or not a person is one to whom it's worth committing one's life. After the party we all attended, Janice took me to one side and warned me that she felt that Henry and Courtney were just treating us as trophy women."

"I think I know what that means," said Eleanor, "but explain what is Janice's take on the term."

"Janice thinks that some men choose to be seen with women for whom they've no special feelings of affection but women whom other men will see as attractive. The other men will then feel a degree of envy towards the men to whom the women seem to be attached. The expensive brooches are all part of this, *'Look what I can afford to deck out my woman with'.*"

"So we're just trophy women, there to adorn our man and enhance his reputation."

"That's just about the size of it," said Elizabeth. "When my parents came up to London recently, I introduced them to Henry. After meeting him, my mother took me to one side and told me she just didn't take to Henry although she couldn't rationalise and put her finger on why she felt that way. We should have recognised the dangers of dating apparently glamourous men from our friend, Joan's, experience. We were all a bit jealous of her when she married that dashing cavalry officer who served with the Life Guards and was in line to inherit a peerage but their marriage became unstuck when she discovered he was a notorious womaniser and serial adulterer!"

"Well, Henry and Courtney don't seem to be that sort of womaniser but we now have a new situation in which the pair of them seem to be in some danger, so much so, they've moved out of their office on Oakenhampton, changed their phones, moved into secret accommodation and don't seem particularly keen to get in touch with us again. I'm sure this sense of danger must have come about when that young man, Hamish, who worked in their office, was murdered. According to the papers, he didn't turn up for work but drove to the White Hart on the Stow Road where he called in for a drink, abandoned his car in the pub car park and was found buried next to a nearby layby. He'd been shot! Perhaps Henry and Courtney think they are targets for the same murderer. I don't fancy continuing a relationship with someone living under this sort of threat."

"Neither do I, but they've arranged this date for tomorrow," observed Elizabeth. "I feel like breaking off our relationship then and handing Henry back this brooch."

"Yes, I feel much the same," said Eleanor. "The worst part of any relationship is when the time comes to break it off without being able to give our friend any acceptable reason for doing so, but if the chemistry's wrong, we know the relationship can't be sustained."

"We've both had relationships we've had to finish because it became obvious that the man was not interested in marriage but just sex," stated Elizabeth, "but those were the easy relationships to terminate."

"The fact that it appears that neither Henry nor Courtney are prepared to attend church with us is also a negative pointer," observed Eleanor. "I can't imagine sharing life with someone who doesn't share my faith."

"It was remiss of us not to have checked this out when we met at the dating agency," said Elizabeth, "but Henry was so full of what he wanted to tell me about himself that I just didn't have an opportunity to fit this in."

Elizabeth had a flat in South Kensington and Eleanor had a similar apartment in Chelsea. They both attended an Anglican church, overshadowed by a much larger

Roman Catholic church. Their church. Holy Trinity, Brompton, was right next to the Brompton Oratory.

Eleanor looked at her watch.

"We must be getting back to our offices. I'll call for you tomorrow and we can make our way together to 'The Snow Leopard'. Perhaps we'll learn a bit more about the danger that Henry and Courtney seem to think they're in."

Chapter 12

<u>Issues Resolved</u>

That Wednesday evening, the team of police officers which Superintendent Colin Whittaker had organised for the arrest at the Snow Leopard, were in position. A couple of officers, who had been advised to dress smartly for the job in hand at this particular venue, had a table reserved near the one which had been booked by Henry and Courtney. They were in place by 6:30 p.m. Christine and Bill were waiting in an unmarked police car with Colin in the Snow Leopard car park near another unmarked police car, occupied by two more police officers. Elizabeth and Eleanor arrived at 6:45 p.m., dressed in their finery and oblivious of the police presence. They were shown to the table booked by Henry and Courtney and took their places. They declined the offer of drinks until their gentlemen friends arrived. At 6:55 p.m., Courtney's BMW drove into the car park, but no, it wasn't Courtney's vehicle, it had the wrong registration number, but yes, it clearly was his vehicle. He and Henry were seen to alight, once the car had been parked. Courtney had clearly been driving on false number plates! Courtney and Henry were dressed in smart evening dress. It was the sort of restaurant where a lounge suit and tie were barely acceptable attire when dining during the evening.

Christine and Bill felt their tension rise. After a very few minutes, Colin received a buzz on his phone which indicated that all was set. Christine and Bill left the car and strode into the restaurant. They were expected by the Maitre d'Hotel who pointed out the table occupied by Courtney and Henry with their guests. They made their way to the table. Christine showed her warrant card and identified herself and her colleague. She cautioned them in a confident voice.

"Henry Ericson and Courtney Cavendish, I am arresting you on suspicion of the murder of Hamish McIntosh, You do not have to say anything, but it may harm your defence if you do not mention when questioned something that you rely on in court. Anything you do say may be given in evidence."

Silence descended on the restaurant. Henry and Courtney stood and were meekly led away. The back up team was not needed to enforce this arrest. After a while, conversation started up on the other tables but for quite some time, Elizabeth and Eleanor remained in stunned silence. They felt deeply self-conscious as they thought that the eyes of all those on nearby tables would be on them. What were they all thinking? 'Are these two a pair of gangsters' molls?'

After a few minutes, Eleanor picked up Courtney's credit card which he'd put on the table as he arrived and sat down.

"Well," she said to Elizabeth as she recovered from her state of shock, "while we're here, we may as well take advantage of the fare on offer but I don't want to continue sitting here under the curious gaze of those nearby."

She summoned a waiter and requested that they should be re-seated at a table for two on the other side of the restaurant. The waiter complied with this request.

Once re-seated, they ordered a glass of wine each and scrutinised the menus they had been handed.

"Doesn't that explain everything," said Elizabeth, still a bit breathless from the impact of receiving the unexpected revelation of Henry and Courtney's misdeed. "The murder of Hamish and their telling us they've gone to ground because they were in danger."

"Not everything," answered Eleanor. "Why would they have murdered Hamish? I suppose all that will become clear in due course."

"I noticed that you picked up Courtney's credit card," said Elizabeth, "but it's unlikely we'll be able to order anything in the contactless range here. I imagine the wine we've just ordered will have already taken us past the contactless limit."

"No worry," replied Eleanor. "I know Courtney's pin number."

"However do you remember that?" asked Elizabeth who was quite incredulous.

"Courtney has no fewer than four credit cards," explained Eleanor. "He told me that the pin number for each card is the date of a famous battle with the same initial as the bank. For the Halifax, it's Hastings, 1066, for the National Westminster, it's Waterloo, 1815, for Santander its Saratoga, 1777, and for Barclays its Blenheim, 1704. The card left on the table was a Barclay card."

"Lucky it wasn't the NatWest," joked Elizabeth. "You might have entered the date of the Battle of Naseby."

They placed their order and the conversation which followed was largely speculation on why and how Henry and Courtney had murdered Hamish McIntosh.

"While we now know why they went out of view for a while," commented Elizabeth, "I wonder however did the police track them down to here?"

"I had really expected that I would have to tell Courtney that we needed to end our relationship this evening," said Eleanor, "and hand him back this brooch."

"It looks as if the relationships have been ended without our having to break them ourselves," said Elizabeth, "which I think is a great relief for both of us."

Meanwhile, the two officers who'd been recruited as part of the police backup team took advantage of the fact that they were here on police business and entitled to expenses. They ordered themselves steak for their main course and sherry trifle for their sweet.

The police had no difficulty in proving their case against Henry and Courtney. Mr Grimond was asked to attend an identification process in which Courtney and Henry stood, separated by three other men. Ten men had been selected because they were similar in appearance to Henry and Courtney. Mr. Grimond observed the individuals from behind a screen and immediately reacted as he came to Courtney.

"That's him," he triumphantly exclaimed.

Christine noticed that Courtney did have a small V shaped scar above his left eyebrow which Mr Grimond had mentioned earlier.

Although the steering wheel in Hamish's car had been wiped clean, there were enough of Henry and Courtney's fingerprints on other parts of the car to indicate that they had been in the car. This fact had already been verified from fingerprints left on the cylindrical slide rule which Christine had taken to their office to be handled by Henry and Courtney but fresh fingerprints were taken of the couple after they'd been arrested. Henry and Courtney couldn't offer any plausible reason why their fingerprints should have been found in Hamish's car. The discovery made at the Chiltern and Cotswold Bank now enabled them to prove the computer hacking activities which Hamish had been clearly threatening to expose.

A search of the accommodation where the couple were now living revealed the gun which ballistics proved to be the murder weapon.

With so much conclusive evidence against Henry and Courtney, it didn't take the jury long to come back with a guilty verdict. The police were commended on the way they'd handled this investigation. Henry and Courtney were given life sentences but as a result of their early 'guilty' plea, these were lighter than they might have been. Henry and Courtney revealed how the money they had accumulated from their computer scam could be retrieved. Restoration was made to the affected parties.

Why was it that the computer fraud took so long to unearth? It only came to light as a result of the information Christine had picked up when she visited Mrs Boyd. The entries on a bank statement, apparently recording payments made to a public utility company, would not necessarily arouse suspicion from anyone whose bank account was comfortably in credit. Indeed, how many of us check that we're not paying standing orders and direct debits beyond the time when such payments are no longer required?

Why were receipts sent out to those being scammed? Henry and Courtney had argued that if any of these payments had been made from small businesses or local authorities who were included among the victims of this scam, then their accounts would be regularly audited. Absence of a receipt for a payment would result in further investigation which would lead to the risk of the scam being uncovered.

The victim's parents couldn't be recompensed for this crime. They would never get over the loss of Hamish, a son of whom they were so proud. Some small relief for their grief came about as a result of their taking in a teenage Ukrainian refugee who had been rescued, unharmed, from an apartment building in Kiev which had been hit by a Russian missile. Both his parents had been killed but Mr and Mrs McIntosh became his good substitute parents, taking great pleasure in acclimatising the Ukrainian lad into the English way of life and ensuring he had a good education.

Christine and Bill paid another visit to the Chiltern and Cotswold Bank to point out to Mr Padbury how the bank's security could be improved. One-time verification codes should not just be sent to a customer's mobile phone before a transaction can go through but also, before any personal data can be changed. This will prevent a mobile phone number being temporarily changed by a hacker to substitute his own number before making a transaction.

When Christine next visited Canterbury's supermarket, she was met by a very happy looking Jeremy Kimber who proudly showed the changes the top management had made to the self-checkout area. Items to be scanned were brought into the area in bags in the trolleys, the bags transferred on to an input scale pan and items scanned as they were transferred to the output pan. The decrease in weight as the item was removed from the input pan and the increase in weight as the item was put on the output pan were checked by the computer system to see that they were the same and corresponded with the weight registered for the item on the data base which showed up as the item was scanned.

"This system has significantly reduced the loss we were making through shoplifting," Mr Kimber reported to Christine.

When Christine and Michael called on Mrs. Boyd to return her laptop, they found her and the children looking much happier. The dog was much healthier now as a result of the tablets which Michael had provided. The knowledge that she would no longer be paying out £200 a month for no good reason coupled with knowing that the money which the hackers had taken would soon be restored, left Mrs. Boyd confident that she could now budget in a way which would enable them all to eat well including the dog.

"Do you leave your computer powered up, even when you're not actually using it?" Bill asked Mrs Boyd.

"Well yes," said Mrs. Boyd, looking worried that they were going to tell her that this was bad practice.

Seeing her worried look, Christine spoke to reassure Mrs. Boyd.

"Nothing wrong in that. Most people leave their computers continuously running, even when not in use but do you have any anti-virus software installed?"

Mrs Boyd had to admit she hadn't.

"Did you do the history quiz which came up some time ago on the Microsoft Network home page?" asked Bill.

"I probably did. I enjoy having a go at these quizzes although I'm afraid that I don't do very well at them," Mrs. Boyd replied, "but I feel that I'm learning something when the answers come up later."

Christine and Bill then explained to Mrs Boyd what the Cyber Crime department had come up with when they examined her computer. She was relieved to know that the offending trojan had been cleared. Christine recommended antimalware software that Mrs. Boyd shouldn't delay in getting installed on all the computers in the house, the children's laptops as well as her own and suggested a package which would be suitable.

"This software will safeguard not just one but all the devices in the house used for communication, including your mobile phone," she explained.

Michael, Christine and Richard visited the puppy farm in Simbourne and were pleased to discover that the owner had properly registered his business. He seemed genuinely pleased to take them to the back of the house where everything was looking much cleaner and hygienic as a result of improvements he had been required to make.

Bill gave some thought to the fact that Henry and Courtney had driven round with false number plates to avoid being picked up by a patrol car and this probably delayed their arrest. Driving with false number plates is a serious offence, especially as it could hinder the apprehension of a hit and run driver who had caused an accident. Bill knew that there were more drivers using false number plates than the police may have realised. Such drivers are unlikely to be apprehended except in a case where they are involved in a serious accident and many drivers are prepared to take what they consider to be a small risk. False number plates not only disguise a car of interest from police patrol cars but enable congestion zones in busy cities like London to be entered without leaving the trace which is needed to obtain payment. Bill came up with the idea that number plates should be made to incorporate a GPS (Global Positioning System) chip which uniquely related to the car registered and was connected to the car's electronics so that the car would be immobilised if the number plate was removed. Such a chip would also be invaluable in locating a stolen car or a car involved in a crime. While many cars do incorporate such a GPS chip, they are not integrated into the number plate.

Olivia soon found herself another job and a few weeks later, she announced her engagement to the son of the local dentist.

There was good news on the romantic front for Elizabeth and Eleanor. Elizabeth married an accountant and Eleanor, a lecturer at University College, London University. They were both young men who attended their church of Holy Trinity, Brompton.

"I feel so happy and very much loved," confessed Eleanor to Elizabeth. "Why ever did we go to that dating agency when there were such lovely men in plain sight at our church?"

I've saved the most important piece of news for the end. Christine married her vet friend, Michael, and they now have two lovely children, a boy and a girl.

"I just can't understand why it took me so long to get myself seriously romantically involved with such a lovely, intelligent and resourceful young woman," Michael thought to himself. "The fact she's nearly four years older than myself doesn't matter one little bit!"

APPENDIX 1

Self-Checkout Till Control Programme

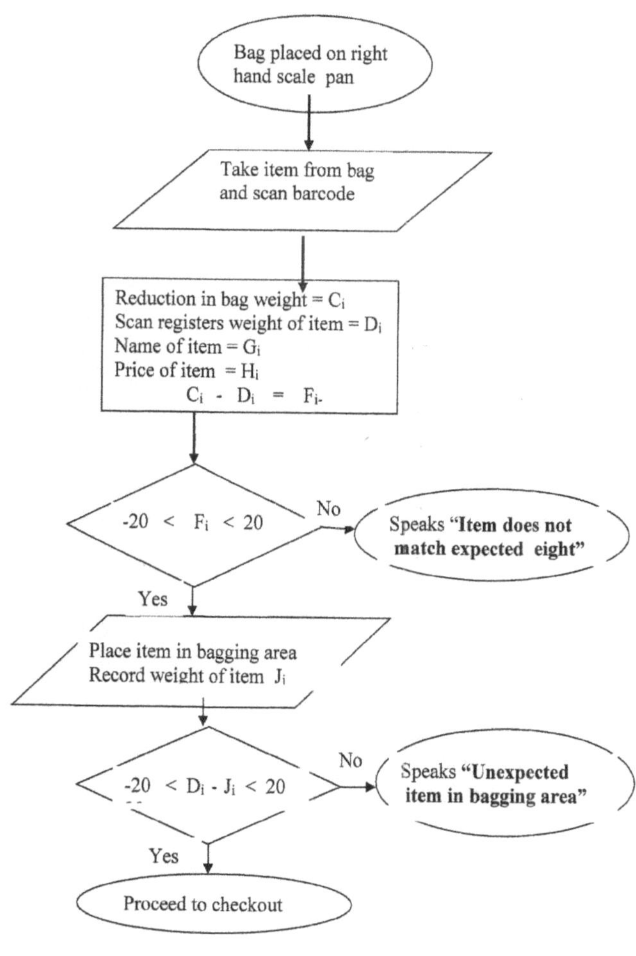

	Computer Input	Computer Action	A	B	C	D	E	F	G	H	I
			0	0	0	0	0	0	0	0	0
1											
2	Bag placed on input scale pan	Records bag weight in A	15,786								
"	"	"	"	"	"	"	"	"	"	"	"
"	"	"	"	"	"	"	"	"	"	"	"
"	"	"	"	"	"	"	"	"	"	"	"
301	Previous transaction completed	Current bag weight recorded in A	11,507								
302	Jar of Ginger Jam taken from bag	Records new bag weight in B		11,010							
303		A - B in C			497						
304											
305	Barcode on Jar of Ginger Jam scanned	Records Name of Item in G								Ginger Jam	
306		Records cost of item in H									£1.71
307		Records weight of item in D				495					
308		C - D in F						2			
309		If -20 < F < 20 0 in G else 1 in G							0		
309		If 0 in G go to 311, if 1 in G, go to 10,000									
310											
311	Jar of Ginger Jam placed in bagging area	Records weight of item in E					497				
312		C - E in F						0			
313		If -20 < F < 20 0 in G else 1 in G							0		
314		If 0 in G go to 316, if 1 in G, go to 10,001									
315											
316	Take next item from input scale pan	Repeats lines 301 t0 314									
317	"	"	"	"	"	"	"	"	"	"	"
318	"	"	"	"	"	"	"	"	"	"	"
	"	"	"	"	"	"	"	"	"	"	"
9,000	Customer indicates he wishes to checkout	Costs in I summed and displayed									
9,001	Customer pays sum rerquired	Printout generated listing items, prices and total cost.									
	"	"	"	"	"	"	"	"	"	"	"
	"	"	"	"	"	"	"	"	"	"	"
	"	"	"	"	"	"	"	"	"	"	"
10,000		**'Item doesn't match expected weight' is spoken aloud**									
		'Unexpected item in bagging area'									

APPENDIX 2

Then ABCD of Salvation

After Marion had approved Sydney's idea of using two mini food supply hub volunteers to work as a pair and lead a spiritual conversation with members of a family attending a lunch put on by the mini food supply hub during school holidays, Sydney and Michael led such a conversation. The following script closely reports the conversation they held with Arnold and Jackie Glazier over coffee which was served after the main meal when the children had gone to join the play activities arranged for them.

Michael :-   Sydney, you were telling me that you were certain that you were going to heaven!

Arnold :-   No-one can be certain of that.

Michael :-   People hearing you say that, Sydney, may think you're very arrogant and self-righteous, someone who thinks he is better than most of those around him.

Sydney :-   Whatever people may think, just the opposite is the case. The reason that I feel certain that I'll go to heaven is that I know I'm unworthy. If you knew all the sin in my life, the wrong things I've said, the lies

I've told, the people whom I've let down, the evil thoughts which run through my mind, the important things I should have done to help others and didn't, well, if you knew all this, you wouldn't want to be my friend.

Jackie :-	Well, if all this is true about yourself, it sounds as if you've disqualified yourself from going to heaven so why ever do you think otherwise?

Sydney :-	Because that's something Jesus promised. When Jesus was on earth, he said and did things which proved beyond all reasonable doubt that he was God, living on earth in human form. He even predicted his own death and resurrection.

Arnold :-	Although all that's in the Bible, it's not necessarily true, is it?

Michael :-	Great scholars, yes, even those who were extremely sceptical about the resurrection have carefully examined the evidence and come to the conclusion that, yes, there is no doubt that Jesus lived, was crucified and rose again as a real and living person! Some have described this as the best attested fact in history.

Jackie :-   Yes, but that doesn't mean that you, Sydney, will rise from the dead too and end up in heaven.

Sydney :-   If Jesus was God, and there is no doubt, not just in my mind that he was, but also in the minds of most intelligent people I know, then he is the most important thing in the universe. We must carefully heed what he said and recognise that it must be true.

Michael :-   Jesus' disciples were amazed to find that a rich young ruler was disqualified from heaven, even though he had obeyed the commandments. They had thought that wealth was a sign of being specially favoured by God, but Jesus went on to say that it is humanly impossible to get to heaven!

Arnold :-   So there you are then, if Jesus said it is impossible to get to heaven, why can you be so confident of going there.

Sydney :-   If we consider the whole of what Jesus

said, he continued by saying that although getting to heaven was impossible for man, all things are possible to God.

Michael :-   So how then does God get you to heaven.

Sydney :-   When I described all that was wrong in my life, you jumped to the conclusion that I hadn't lived the extremely good life that is necessary to earn my place in heaven, but in reality, it's not enough just to lead a very good life, because God is perfect and you have to be perfect to come into God's presence. No-one is that perfect in their own strength.

Michael :-   So, how does God enable you to enter heaven?

Sydney :-   By taking all the sin which would otherwise disqualify me from heaven upon himself. He did this as he died on the cross and suffered the punishment which I deserved for my sins. If he took my sin away, then doesn't that leave me perfect with no sin to answer for? If I'm perfect, then I can enter heaven with the same status as any who are already there.

Indeed, better than that, Jesus said that we would have the status of being one of his brothers or sisters. That is what is meant by saying that we will become God's children by adoption and grace.

Michael :- So then, you're saying that to be sure of entering heaven, you need to ACKNOWLEDGE your own sinfulness and BELIEVE that Jesus died to take that sin on himself. Is that all there is to it?

Sydney :- No, a response is called for. You must COMMIT yourself to speaking words and thinking thoughts which acknowledge that Jesus has done this, and finally, you must DEDICATE your life to Jesus.

Michael :- That sounds like an ABCD, Accept, Believe, Commit and Dedicate, but how do you dedicate your life to Jesus?

Sydney :- I follow the acronym, WWJD, 'What would Jesus Do?' Whatever situation I'm in, should a dilemma arise requiring a decision, I ask myself, 'What would Jesus have done in this situation?'

Arnold :-   What about all those who follow other religions? They may not accept Jesus but they worship the same God as you!

Sydney :-   I don't believe they do. The Islamic extremists believe in a God who, among other things, considers that if a person is born into a Moslem family and initially accepts Islamic beliefs, then decides later to reject Islam, he should be executed. They believe that women are inferior and should not receive the same education as men. This is certainly not my God and neither can the God of the Jews be my God because they rejected him and had him executed two thousand years ago.

Arnold :-   What about moderate Moslems, good Jews, indeed, any person who is good but who doesn't accept Jesus? Won't they go to heaven?

Sydney :-   I can't give a definite answer to this. All I can say is that God is a perfectly just and loving God who wouldn't do anything we regarded as a subhuman form of justice. However, only those who have accepted Jesus as Saviour have the assurance of going to heaven with the status of being an adopted child of God. Indeed, anyone arriving at the gates of heaven with the attitude that I've lived such a good life that I deserve to get in, hasn't appreciated the enormous cost in the suffering that Jesus endured to buy his loved ones a place in heaven. It would be rather like a guest at the end of a lavish banquet going up to the host and offering 10p to pay for his share of the food.

We must bear in mind that Jesus said, 'I am the way, the truth and the life. No-one comes to the Father except by me.'

Michael :- Have you found dedicating your life to Jesus to have been very restrictive to your lifestyle?

Sydney :- On the contrary, I have felt a freedom, a joy in life and a purpose for living which I never had before. My relationships with others have improved. I see new meanings in things and events to which I previously paid little attention and I am conscious of the continued presence of Jesus as a very real but unseen friend.

Arnold and Jackie Glazier went away in a thoughtful frame of mind.

APPENDIX 3

Police Officer Badges of Rank

Constable   Sergeant   Inspector   Chief Inspector   Super-intendent

Chief Super-intendent   Assistant Chief Constable   Deputy Chief Constable   Chief Constable

APPENDIX 4

List of Characters

Arnold Glazier	Beneficiary of St. Giles Church Mini Food Supply Hub
Bill Matthews	Detective Sergeant, Christine Power's partner
Christine Powers	Detective Inspector based at Oakenhampton
Colin Whittaker	Chief Inspector at Oakenhampton Police Station
Courtney Cavendish	Director of C & E Software Enterprises
Eleanor Pedlingham	Courtney Cavendish's girlfriend
Elizabeth Draycott	Henry Erikson's girlfriend
George Apsley	Inspector from Police Cyber Crime Division
Hamish McIntosh	Software expert working at C & E Software
Henry Erikson	Courtney's partner & Director of C & E Software
Jackie Glazier	Arnold Glazier's wife

Janice   Mutual friend of Eleanor
                           and Elizabeth
Jenifer Boyd   Mrs. Boyd's daughter
Jeremy Kimber   Manager of Canterbury's
                           supermarket
Joan   Mutual friend of Eleanor
                           and Elizabeth
Marion Attwood   Organizer of St. Giles
                           Church Mini Food Supply
                           Hub
Michael Lapworth   Vet and Christine's friend
Mr. Grimond   Manager of White Hart Pub.
Mr. McIntosh   Hamish's father
Mr. Padbury   Manager of branch of
                           Chiltern & Cotswold Bank
Mrs. Boyd   Impoverished inhabitant of
                           Oakenhampton
Mrs. McIntosh   Hamish's mother
Olivia Clark   Clerical assistant at C & E
                           Software Enterprises
Richard Carstairs   RSPCA Inspector
Stuart Boyd   Mrs. Boyd's son
Sydney Kenyon   Churchwarden at St. Giles
                           Church, Oakenhampton

The books published by Midhurst have been written by Dr Ray Filby who has had many years' experience of church life in a number of churches, fulfilling at various times the roles of Pathfinder Group Leader, Youth Fellowship Leader, Secretary to the Parochial Church Council, Churchwarden and Reader (Licensed Lay Minister). This experience is reflected in the stories he writes which embrace several genres, including historical fiction, short stories, Bible study, murder stories and romantic fiction. They are all available from Amazon in paperback or Kindle form.

The Sun and the Moon of Alexandria

This is a fictional biopic of Apollos, a missionary saint and one of St. Paul's co-workers. Although mentioned many times in the New Testament, little is known of the life and background of Apollos. Thus, there is scope to create a story which constructs a feasible account of Apollos' youth in Egypt, his journey to Israel, his conversion, his relationship with St. Paul, his missionary work and his marriage. The story culminates in his martyrdom. In situations where Apollos interacts with well-known Biblical characters, the narrative remains faithful to the New Testament account.

(This book is published by the Book Guild)

Parables, the Greatest Stories ever told - Retold

'The Greatest Stories ever told – Retold' focuses on the better known parables of Jesus and rewrites them as situations in modern life which correspond to the situations in Jesus' day, attempting to promote the same teaching that Jesus was giving in the original parable. Each parable is preceded by a modern translation of the original parable and followed by ten questions which are suitable for a person's private devotions or for use in the context of a group Bible study.

St. Columba's – Its Life and Its People

Churches are living organisms, each with their own distinctive patterns of life. While their members experience the same ups and downs in life as the population as a whole, their Christian faith results in their reacting to circumstances in a distinctive way.

This book is a set of short stories, some of which trace the unfolding of events which occur as part of church life, and others which recount the experience of individual church members. Readers are invited to consider the practical or ethical problems which arise in these stories and think how they themselves might have dealt with or reacted to these situations.

The Countess who should have been Queen

Margaret Plantagenet was born near the end of the Wars of the Roses. As the daughter of the brother of King Edward IV, a situation could well have arisen when she or her brother, Edward, had a claim to the throne. Margaret was not ambitious to become Queen but was happy to marry a commoner and settled as an enlightened landowner with her husband in Berkshire. Margaret became Queen Catherine of Aragon's chief lady-in-waiting and was awarded a peerage to become Countess of Salisbury. Margaret faithfully supported Catherine right through her reign and as far as she could when Catherine was sent to live in isolation after her divorce. One of Margaret's sons, Reginald, became a prominent churchman and angered the King by writing a treatise, heavily critical of Henry VIII, the way he had divorced Catherine and taken over the Church of England. Reginald was living out of reach of Henry on the continent so Henry vented his wrath on Margaret and her family.

Consequences of Immature Love

Boy-Girl, Man-Woman relationships cement our society. Because these relationships are seldom straightforward, they provide scope for an indefinite number of works of fiction. In this novel, you are invited to follow the amorous adventures of Georgina Matthews and Arthur Gray from the time they leave school and start at university until they ultimately marry the partner for whom they seemed destined from the outset.

The story told might be of special interest to a young person embarking on the minefield of love and courtship as they consider the factors which led to the success or failure of the relationships encountered in this novel. Ethical factors are involved and it is significant that a shared Christian faith led to the final happy outcome.

Soldiers, Saints and Sinners

'*Soldiers, Saints and Sinners*' is a collection of fictitious stories, featuring some of the minor characters whom Jesus encountered in his ministry. It attempts to suggest how their backgrounds might have been important in the way they led to their encounter with Jesus and the way these encounters furthered the progress of Jesus' ministry. Each story is preceded by a modern Biblical translation of the passage which recounts their appearance on the scene where Jesus was ministering and is followed by five questions which are suitable for a person's private devotions or for use in the context of a group Bible study.

The Tasks of Chronavon

When sensible twelve-year-olds, Alfred and Alice meet a mysterious angel called Chronavon in the vestry of their church, it seems someone is playing a practical joke on them. After all, angels don't just pop up in church vestries to enlist the help of two young people to journey back in time to prevent a devilish time traveller from altering the course of history. Yet it soon becomes clear that Chronavon's incredible story is true. As Alfred and Alice are whisked backwards through the centuries, they become immersed in the rich customs and costumes of the past through Henry III's troubled reign, the insecurity of Princess Elizabeth before she became Queen Elizabeth I and the Civil War between the Cavaliers and Roundheads. 'The Tasks of Chronavon' is an exciting, informative tale for young readers which effortlessly weaves fact and fiction with a sprinkling of humour and shows how little human values have changed over time.

The Evil Occupants of Easingdale Castle

Teenager, Jason, and his friends, Bill, Becky and Liz, are recruited by an unusual messenger to pit their wits against an international gang of forgers, occupying their local castle. The gang are intent on destabilising the British economy by flooding the country with forged £20 notes which could pass off as the real thing. The gang is well equipped with hi-tech machines.

It remains to be seen whether Jason and his friends, who are also technically knowledgeable, can outwit the gang.

Technology will have advanced since this book was written and young readers are invited to consider whether they could have done better than Jason and his friends with equipment now available.

The Evil Emir of Transoxiana

Becky meets with her special friends, Jason, Bill and Liz, to tell them she is being posted to Transoxiana. She needs to explain exactly where she will be working, that she will be accompanied by Jason and that she will be spending some time with her Kyrgyz penfriend, Askari, and her husband, Temier.

During Becky's stay with Askari, Temier falls foul of an extremist Islamic cleric, the self-styled, Emir of Transoxiana. The resourcefulness of Becky and Jason, helped by Bill and Liz who travel out to join them, is needed to keep Askari and Temier safe from the Evil Emir. In spite of the danger being faced, they all manage to have the experiences in Transoxiana which make their stay both exciting and enjoyable.

A Church like Cluedo

After graduating from college as a civil engineer, Annette Owen had hoped to work in the developing world under the auspices of a missionary society. When this door to Christian service was closed, she applied to become an ordained minister but was turned down by the selection committee. She was however able to exercise a very fulfilled ministry as a clergy wife. Unfortunately, her clergy husband had dark secrets in his life of which Annette was totally unaware until a situation arose which resulted in murder being committed. The impact of this had an unexpected effect on the course of Annette's life.

Inspector Sinclair and Sergeant Powers' most interesting cases

This account of some interesting cases solved by the detective duo, Inspector Sinclair and Sergeant Powers, is not a normal 'whodunnit' in which the murderer is not revealed until the very end when the detective reveals the clues which he or she alone has picked up to solve the case without sharing their significance with the reader until the very end.

The stories in this book are divided into sections, a list of those involved to help the reader keep track of the characters,

'the Event' which describes the situation when the murder took place,

'the Investigation' which describes the systematic way in which the detectives investigated the case and

'the Evidence' in which the crucial evidence by which a cast iron case against the murderer was built up, is reviewed.

An Insight into the Gospels and the Book of Acts

'An Insight into the Gospels and the Book of Acts' is an overview of the themes, contents, emphases, and structure of the first five books of the New Testament. While there is so much similarity in the stories and teaching in each of the gospels, this book contrasts the way each gospel is written and presented. It highlights the quite remarkable differences which exist between each of the gospels as they are directed to different audiences and have different primary objectives. The book is presented with the main content of the book appearing on the right hand (odd numbered) pages and supportive texts placed opposite the relevant passages on the left hand pages.

The Warrior and the Bride

This work of Biblical fiction is largely set in the period covered by the 2nd Book of Samuel and the 1st Book of Kings. It features Benaiah and Abishag, two characters who had important roles to play in serving King David and his successor. Although a work of fiction, the author has tried to make it consistent with the Biblical narrative and references are provided wherever the story is related to a Biblical event. The author realises that minor inconsistencies occur in the text but then, minor inconsistencies can be found in the Bible itself. There is no indication in the Bible that the two main characters were in any way related but nothing in the Bible specifically states that they were not.

Puzzles, Quiz and Activities Suitable for Social Events
Volumes 1, 2, 3 & 4

These books consist of a set of puzzles, quiz and activities which the author designed for use at a monthly social event organised by St. Michael's, Church, Budbrooke, in the Community Centre in the part of the parish known as Chase Meadow. People who have opted to take part really seem to have enjoyed these activities which are interesting rather than extremely challenging. While a good general knowledge is helpful in completing some of the activities, they are not designed to expose people's ignorance as data sheets and appropriate reference books like atlases are made available to help participants find any information needed. Thus, the activities are educational.

The socials run at Chase Meadow are not restricted to church members but all and sundry are invited as part of the church outreach. With many of the activities, a final stage often involves deciphering a phrase, quote or saying. As the socials are sponsored by the church, many of the quotes to be deciphered are Biblical texts. However, anyone choosing to use these ideas could quite easily modify the final stage and use a secular quote rather than a Biblical text to be deciphered.